GRAY

DAWN MOORE ROY

MIDDLESEX
PRESS

MIDDLESEX
PRESS

Boston, Massachusetts

Copyright © 2021 by Dawn Moore Roy

Hardcover ISBN 978-1-7375166-0-6
eBook ISBN 978-1-7375166-1-3

Library of Congress Control Number: 2021913969

Book production by The Pub Pros, Inc., www.thepubpros.com
Cover and interior design by Zoe Norvell

Printed and bound in the United States of America.

FOR MICHAEL

ACKNOWLEDGMENTS

I cannot begin to express my thanks to the publishers at the Pub Pros. Through the entire process, my experience with co-founders Celia Blue Johnson and Maria Gagliano has been nothing short of, as Celia would say, "lovely." My copyeditor, Beth Blachman, taught me a few new punctuation rules that I will never break again! And a thank you to Zoe Norvell who designed the book cover, jacket, and interior, then wrapped it all up together for us with a most beautiful original design. My photographer, Stacey Maddox, was especially patient with me and actually managed to take some great natural photographs. Niki Papadopoulos for her verification of the Greek colloquialisms. And a very special shout-out to my professors and classmates at the University of Edinburgh, who provided me with the kind of formative feedback that a writer could only dream about. And, of course, a special thanks to my loving family and close friends who have encouraged me to write a story that is playful, but that also weaves in things that matter.

I would be remiss not to include the great author Virginia Woolf, who first made me want to pick up a pen and write.

What a man knows, he must do.

—A. H. Maslow,
Motivation and Personality

CHAPTER 1

THRESHOLD

We don't have complete emotions about the present,
only about the past.

—Virginia Woolf, *A Writer's Diary*

No one knew how long it would take. Least of all Vera. It was the cusp of a late summer and the beginning of a colorful New England fall. Her car windows were wide open and without that pesky glare from headlights following her, Vera decided to take her time. She crept along the drift and curl of narrow roads, lined with the mighty branches of century-old trees, and beneath this canopy of floating red and orange leaves, she longed for the trees' age-old wisdom and stability. Right. That isn't going to happen, she told herself. Just speed it up. The coolness of a dark breeze hit her in the face hard, and somehow readied her for the coming prickling jolt, the wave of her own salty sweat, and Vera had that familiar rush of a new season coming, a big change about to happen.

She strained to hear the chorus of trilling crickets, and, with surprise, heard the soft talk of an owl. The orchestration, the fluidity of the roads soothed her, delivered her, and she was suddenly standing in the doorway of hospital room 350.

Jesus. Look at him.

Vera had considered a sometimes-effective practice in Buddhism—imagining a situation before it happens. She would have been familiar with, prepared for the pitiable sight of her dying father. Nonetheless, this approach wouldn't have worked anyway, because the vision of her father's death—anyone's death, really—bordered on hopeful fantasy: the departing tucked in bed with stiff white sheets; people circled around the bed dreamily holding hands; the air laced with the sugary breath of merciful angels. Plus, Vera had never been a totally committed Buddhist anyway.

Vera sniffed, and her nostrils caught the sting of disinfectant roaming throughout the air, the tiny particles stumbling over one another to find a way out. Warren sat propped up—the image of an overgrown baby in a highchair flashed by. God, she hated her thoughts sometimes.

His now crumpled frame was held in place (more like tied up) with white cotton straps attached to a lime-green leatherette lounger (easy to wipe down with antiseptic, a nurse might say). Hitting at the chest, a large, curved plastic tray helped to keep him upright. Jesus Christ. Warren. Once a man with presence, her father seemed a complete stranger. A foggy drifter cast away: roped and bobbing on the unpredictability of a colorless sea—tethered between a life and a death.

Pausing, she looked up to the white ceiling. Lost herself in the swirl of infinitesimal blue specks. It was an oddity about her (funny, really), and Max—poor, dear, dead Max—would sometimes comment about it when they were married. "I don't know of anyone else who looks up so much," he'd say adoringly to her when they were alone. He was good at that, being so sweet, so attentive when no one else was around. "What are you looking for up there, my love?" he'd say, and cock his head, touch her with his soft, flirty eyes. Velvet eyes. Max had velvet eyes.

Vera treated every room in every building like an open sky. Chin up, she'd talk, work, make love even, with one eye on the ceiling above. "Keep your chin up, love." Those had been Max's last words to her. Before he died in the arms of the bimbo girlfriend.

Stubborn thoughts clogged her head, and she forced a look down. Whispered, "Dad." But the room's ceiling called her back, tempted her with its sheltering sky and bawl of screeching seagulls. And so, again, she looked up.

Recalled the stirring memory of an eagle she once saw. And Vera considered birds in general. Either the prolonged gaze up to the sky, followed with impassioned tales of boldness and strength: of mainsails and massive wings, gliding through a vast blue, with the air brackish and briny, so very clean and fresh. Or—a fleeting glance—the mere blink to the side of the road: the sad spotting of a feathered gray carcass, washed up and dirty, so clearly dead. An imagined whiff—to be sped by quickly and purposefully forgotten. There were few tales of a bird's final journey to death, few recounted sightings of the sick and staggering, from that time between the plume of great glory to the hard fall to a roadside stench.

Drawn in by the sounds of Warren gurgling on phlegm and slow to block her reflex, she looked toward him. Then probed. Yes, it was there. Somehow, this once-grand eagle of a man held on to a small piece of what was.

With care, she examined the ceiling.

Once, on a day sail, she had spotted the sweeping ascent of an albatross while Max was below deck mixing cocktails. Would have been unusual to see such a sizable bird in that part of the Atlantic but she was sure of it. At the time, couldn't remember if it were a sign of good luck or bad.

"Well, if you don't shoot it with a crossbow and hang it around your neck as a burden, I'm kinda sure it's all good," Max had said, and handed her a ridiculously strong, straight-up margarita.

"Otherwise, of course, it would be regrettable for you for the rest of your life." He downed his drink.

She remembered how he had coolly leaned back against the boat's gunnel, as though so proud of this literary association, and fixed his eyes on her—fingering the palm-tree stem of his plastic glass. "So ... it's doom from a figure of speech plucked out of a poem about old mariners ... or the sight of a beautiful bird in flight."

"Another?"

"Well, I'm having one," Max had said, gripping the glossy rungs of the mahogany ladder as he climbed down. He had paused.

"There's always a choice, Vera," he had said. "Your choice." And disappeared down into the galley.

Of course, at this point in the relationship, Vera had already stopped listening to any words of wisdom from Max.

"Go with the beautiful bird," he had yelled from below deck.

Her father gurgled. Without thinking, she blinked and couldn't help but focus on the tiny white bubbles gathering on his lower lip. A few had started the descent. Should she wipe his chin? Should. Should. Holy God.

Instead, she stood frozen. Encased within the solid door frame. Overhead, the bulky molding gave her a sense of protection, the wooden sentries on both sides steadied her legs, and she was surprised to find an effortless comfort from the inanimate. Jesus. And where the hell was Sally.

Eyes squinting, she stared through the room's fluorescent glare to the oversized rectangular window across from her. Searched for anything out there to fix her gaze on. Anything. Nighttime now, too dark to see beyond the glass. The huge window was foggy on the inside and dewy enough to draw on, though. And she had an urge, suddenly, to float across the room, winged like a fairy, pink like a princess, and drag her tiny little finger across the clammy windowpane, carving out a long list of cursive words for her dying father to see and read aloud to her in his strong, soothing voice. Words. How to untangle the swirling new emotions from familiar words.

The best words, the only words she could visualize to scrawl on the steamy hospital window, frightened her. Terrified her. Yet they came to her so easily, so naturally, so very perfectly.

He'll be a stiff, rotting corpse soon. A grand feast of ghastly cold flesh served up buffet style for an army of hungry maggots—that is, if he isn't cremated soon enough, burned to a crisp. And me? My silly self, my fragile shell of skin will live on. Without him.

Words once benign, so harmless in the past, now crystalized

before her in a jagged new form. The edges were sharp, and they cut into her. The words were too personal. Horrifically real, and now personal.

As she stood silent, eyes locked on the window, thoughts about Professor Brody came to mind. He had talked a lot about the word personal. Vera had recently finished up a six-month-long sociology seminar with the famous Sam Brody titled "Self and Society."

Too tall, too thin (running addiction, no doubt), too bald, too excitable and jumpy for her taste, Brody occasionally delivered a shiny penny here and there to his small group (she'd give him that). On occasion, he'd leap to a stand—as if ready to bolt from the room, perhaps considering a short sprint around the block—and, after a lengthy private deliberation, would impart some lasting wisdom or profound question to his little circle of six students (handpicked and all very agreeable and adoring of Professor Brody).

Just take the damn step, Vera said to herself. Walk through the doorway. Walk into the room. But her legs wouldn't move, they felt detached from her body. As if a separate entity.

Professor Brody's pocketful of wisdoms had turned into a game of silently guessing which philosopher he happened to be quoting next—or misquoting. It didn't matter, though, if his personal highs (jogging about in the latest running apparel, or, in seminar, pseudo-reposed in pressed khakis and boat shoes) resulted in self-delusions of champion marathoner or accomplished philosopher; he appeared to be in excellent shape, and the philosophers' thoughts he stole—they were some of the best.

"He's a friendly fool sort of guy … how could anybody not like a guy like that?" Max would have said about him.

Her dad's head jerked forward. The top of his hospital gown caught a sudden stream of thin drool.

Professor Brody rarely gave any author credit at the end of an adage or quote. And only once, through all the seminars did she, during a brief moment of boredom, reflect on the obscenity of the class tuition cost. But, hey. Such a nice guy. To his credit, he did have a few insightful thoughts, though, and one of them had stuck with her.

"*Nosce*, people," Brody had boomed. "*Temet nosce* ... know thyself ... and the only way for you to do this—is to first understand others! We have a newfound worth for the skill ... the gift ... of seeing how one fits in with other people. We have advanced from solitary hunter-gatherer in a cave ... to survival of the fittest in a vast beehive of communication."

At the time, she had glowed within. It was instinctive, entirely characteristic, for her to focus more on others. But then, she never cared much for thinking about herself. Didn't like the banal reality of who she was.

Ms. Vera Mine of Newton, Massachusetts—born, bred, and still there. At fifty-five years old, she considered herself smack in the middle of middle age (after all, it was the early part of the twenty-first century, and she could potentially live to one hundred). Her past included East Coast private schooling (secondary and college), adjunct work as a psychology instructor at one of the lousy local colleges (never evolving into anything permanent), and a divorce two years ago from Max (after twenty some years of marriage).

Warren's eyes were closed, and his chest rose and fell with rapid breaths. Right. He's sleeping now. Having a nice dream. Right.

Like so many, she had been a dreamer—had high aspirations to be somebody: go down in the history books as somehow significant, carry out some remarkable feat for the betterment of all mankind. And she was, just now, beginning to acknowledge this would most likely not happen for her. Or mankind.

She was born to Warren Mine, a decorated American pilot in World War II (medals in the top right drawer of his desk), and an Englishwoman raised in an orphanage, but Vera was never quite sure about the orphanage story. The English part sounded real enough. After her mother divorced Warren and moved out, she left behind pieces of glossy fine bone china, random teacups to stare at, and white doilies to fiddle with. This seemed pretty English.

Her mother was a survivor, not only of the supposed orphanage but of the German Blitz on England, in 1940. Warren verified this. At eight years old, her mother was one of the sole surviving students from the basement of a London elementary school, taken out by the first German aerial bombing. Her mother walked away from the pile of smoldering bricks unscathed, and Warren had bombed the hell out of Berlin two years later. Twenty years after that, Warren met the young beauty over tea while staying in England with distant relatives. They married in 1960 (she eight years younger than he), moved to the States and four months later delivered baby Vera. They divorced when Vera was three, her sister Sally, two.

Warren hacked at the mucus pooling in his throat; the white foam crept down his chin, and she stared at the slow, irregular descent for what seemed an hour. Should she ... where's a facecloth? The ceiling light momentarily caught her eyes. Still, her legs would not move.

Her "mummy" (signature on a card to Vera when she was four) flew back to Europe, speedily remarried, and divorced again. And Vera was always ashamed of this: her mother was a divorcée twice over. Growing up in the middle-class America of the sixties— in a whirl of thrill, with new hopes and dreams; Dr. King, flower power, miniskirts, afros, and bra-burning; against the backdrop of nightly body counts, LA riots, and assassinations—all of it to forever be branded with the glossy black and white photograph of terrified Vietnamese children running from the burn of American napalm—Vera, at ten years old and beyond, could never shake the idea that her mother had divorced twice. She understood this was weird. Shallow.

Vera was a realist, one with little patience for the illusionist, for the bullshitter, yet found herself capable of one self-preserving deception: that the mother she never knew thought about and imagined Vera—what she would have been like—at sixteen, at twenty, at forty. She was certain her mother was regretful and heartbroken for having thrown her daughter to the wind. Vera needed to believe this. And she did.

Mummy's second husband turned out to be another pilot— this one a German named Hans. He died young, and she died shortly thereafter from something no one appeared to be particularly interested in finding out about. Max had always enjoyed referring to Hans as the "Nazi who left your blond bombshell mother a shitload of money." And Max also liked to say, "You're damn lucky she left it all to you and your sister. You know, Vera."

Still standing in the doorway, she pictured her numb legs from afar, her knees frozen solid and straight, holding her up. The air around her suddenly took on the acrid smell of a clogged drain, an unavoidable concoction composed of body, disease, and chemical cleansers—rubs and creams, blood-soaked bandages. Who wouldn't feel nauseous, lightheaded? Sick. Jesus. Help me, God.

Her father's eyes were still closed. The upper part of the hospital gown was drenched, and he was all bolstered upright with rolled towels, except for his head. This part, the head looked disconnected, laid horizontally on its side, on his shoulder. He actively drooled.

A puff of candied perfume engulfed Vera, and she jerked away. Her sister Sally tugged at her, pushed and pulled her through the door into room 350.

And it began. One by one, visitors came and grappled with the juxtaposition; a once awesome presence now reduced to infirmity. So many offered nothing, sometimes only disruption. But there were a few special visitors, too. The ones who made dying a little easier for him. Eye contact was paramount. That, of course, was the fastest way to eliminate those who would not travel with her father to death. But of those who would, their eyes and voices joined together.

CHAPTER 2

DAMN FOOL

The more ways a man is deluded, the happier he is.

—Desiderius Erasmus, *The Praise of Folly*

Day two. Morning. Lying in bed, Warren seemed a bit more alert than he had the day before. You could call it semi-alert: capricious interludes of wakefulness, deep sleep, and everything in between. Vera sat slumped and sore, defeated by her attempts to find a comfortable position on the orange plastic chair with an impossibly curvaceous back. The hospital room played tricks. Took on skewed proportions—grew smaller and stuffier— alarmed her at times with the frightening deception of oxygen slowly being siphoned off. It seemed harder and harder for her to simply take a breath. The word ghoulish floated by, and, like so many other words and visions, it took on new meaning as she stared at her father's ashen, haggard face. An image from a Monet painting popped into her head. One of Claude's few portraits: Claude's wife Camille on her deathbed.

With her back to the hospital window, Vera took note of the warmth from the bright morning sun streaming in and how it gave the room some semblance of a glow. Hope. For what? Speedy death, painless death, a beautiful death, no death. Christ's sake.

Her sister Sally, buffed and puffed, feathered with flair into the room, wearing her new yoga outfit. Vera tried to master the execution of one deep, satisfying breath as Sally interrupted the nurse who was speaking tenderly to Warren about one more cup of crushed ice. Sally talked and walked.

"Hi, Daddy. Bet you're feeling much better today. Brought some magazines. I'll put these gorgeous potted chrysanthemums—I just love this deep color of yellow—over here on the windowsill." She shot a quick smile at Vera.

Was Sally making an effort? Right. Right.

The nurse straightened up and turned, ventured into Sally's eyes—sockets harbored in a starved skull. The nurse's smile faded, and Sally turned to her deep yellow chrysanthemums. From far away, in profile, or better yet from behind, Vera's sister Sally came across as much younger than her age. In a word, spandex. She suspected Sally had an eating disorder but had never discussed this with her sister. It seemed Sally's protruding clavicle was protruding more and more lately. If someone had asked Vera (although no one had) why she never brought this up to her only sister (everyone well aware of the serious consequences of the disease), Vera had a ready answer she couldn't quite explain: You think so? My sister, an eating disorder?

The nurse placed her open hands on Warren's crossed forearms as if to warm his waxen skin, so thinly shelled and delicate now. With exaggerated articulation and the gentle movement of her lips, she whispered: "Warren, I'll leave you for now. If you need me … press the call button … okay?" Waited for him to nod.

From an early life together as sisters, Vera had concluded that Sally found chatter irresistible, and Sally was a true believer in Sally. If anyone were to ask Sally about her partiality toward these characteristics, Vera ventured to guess her sister would be more than delighted to extrapolate on the art of conversation and how it came to her so naturally, conveniently leaving out the small part about how a discussion needed two active participants. It seemed as if Sally were unaware of the people in front of her: talked and talked at the warm bodies as their tepid eyes glazed over. And yet, at other times she suspected Sally, in fact, did see them, and enjoyed keeping them as a polite captive audience through the power of this incessant never-ending natter. Vera vacillated over this.

The nurse left, and Sally sprang into action, prancing about the room. With one quick motion, she perched two inches from Warren's nose and parted her slick cherry lips into a huge toothy smile.

"Daddy, started the best yoga class. Think the instructor likes me ... it's the Ashtanga version. You know—more strenuous than some of the others. Should I ... you know ... be an instructor? I could, I guess. I think I'd be good at it."

Straightening herself up as if suddenly summoned by her potted plant, Sally turned and gazed at the chrysanthemums for some time, frowned as if in deliberation. She continued to talk to the flowers, something about did Warren want a clean pillowcase.

The showy fluttering of Sally's glossed lips caught Vera's attention, and she acknowledged for the first time how large a mouth Sally had: in size, in proportion to the rest of her face, all the more so with Sally's new thinner, more wasted look. Max had once remarked about it before they were married: "Yikes. That sister of yours has a mouth so big you could park my car in it." And followed up with (there was always a follow-up with Max, a clarification he would call it—but in effect a contradiction of sorts): "Of course, I have a small car. I'm not saying Sally's mouth is so big it could handle a van or a school bus. Her mouth isn't *that* big," he had said, and added, "Well ... the van could probably fit." She suddenly missed Max, wished he were there. He could always manage Sally.

Sally dove into the chair next to Warren's bed: the oversized lime-green recliner with padded pleather, wiped clean. Wiggled and flexed about until she rested on a small corner of the seat, and Vera wondered whether the game was to leave as much of the green color exposed as possible—as if at any moment, another lithe figure would appear, and together they'd figure out how to sit together on the seat of a chair designed for one. What a nasty, bitchy thing for me to think. My own sister. Christ.

Edward's appearance was unexpected and brief. An old friend of Warren's, he barely nodded at Vera and Sally, zigzagged to Warren's bedside, and in a state of eye-popping shock, shouted to him about the weather. It was an odd handshake. A short man, with shirt cuffs and pants too long, Edward bowed down to Warren at the bedside, limply shook his dying friend's two middle fingers. "Hi there, Warren! Feeling better? I hope ... sunny and nice out....Yup." Vera suspected if it had been anyone else, Warren would have responded differently to him—harshly—and in a snap, it would all be said. *I'm dying, fool.* But Warren had a soft spot for the Edward Liddles of the world. A gentle understanding. However, she had seen her father publicly dismiss many, watched with a daughter's pride as Warren bravely delivered a blow, a verbal warning, a notice, to a fool here and there. Deserving fools, they were. Yes, deserving.

Warren opened his eyes briefly and smiled. Closed his eyes— as if he didn't care—as if Edward didn't matter so much. Not right now, anyway, as he lay dying. Her father never opened his eyes again while Edward was there. Never spoke to him. Edward scooted out after five minutes.

"Well, that was quick," Sally said. And with a great fuss, she pulled the starched hospital sheet up to Warren's face, flattened out the creases, and patted it again and again around his neck.

"Should we bring in a photo of Mummy for Dad?" Sally said.

"Seriously? I don't think ..."

"I'll bring it," Sally said.

There was only one photo of their mother, and Sally was forever digging up the worn, yellowed wedding photo and parading it around, drawing Vera's attention to it. "I can't believe how much I look like our mother," she'd squeal. "Well, I mean the hair ... looks blond ... and the eyes ... must be blue since she's blond like me." The photo started to corrode with so much handling by Sally, so she had it professionally restored and preserved in a special frame. And her high-pitched teenage revelations evolved into grim and darkly suspicious musings as they grew up: "Hmm ... now you're an adult, Vera, you don't look anything like Mum ... you don't look anything like Dad either. Where did those big gray eyes of yours come from?" This was true. Vera had her own look.

A loud rustle came from the corner as Sally dug through the blue steel locker. She turned her face toward Vera.

"Vera, what are you thinking? It's always so hard to read you. And where are those little slippers? Scuffies or something," she said. "And what about a toothbrush and toothpaste? Where's the nurse?"

Warren gave a weak cough. Barely opened his eyes, as if to see who was there. His tight lips loosened into a sweet, slightly contented smile, and he faded off into what appeared to be sleep. Right. He's sound asleep now. For a little while anyway.

"Found 'em." Sally flapped the pink plastic scuffies in the air. "Wait. I think these scuffies have been used. Aren't these supposed to be in plastic bags? For hygiene's sake? What's Dad supposed to walk in?"

The prattle. The prattle. And from the faintest rumblings, beginning deep inside Vera, there rose a high-pitched screech— a catalyst of sorts—meant for her to stand and scream, to stop Sally. But the screeching, the rumblings quieted to a whimper, and her head went down. Hiding beneath her closed eyelids, a slow, rhythmic ache of sadness strummed through to her ribs and caved inward on itself. Good God.

"At least we have a mirror here," Sally said, and stared into it as if to appraise a face she had never seen before.

Vera loved to look at herself in mirrors. Any mirror she happened to pass by, really. Rationalized this behavior with the idea that she wanted to confirm what Sally repeated over and over: Vera didn't look like Sally, Warren, or her mum … and clarify that her mirror gazing had absolutely nothing to do with narcissism. Right. Right.

Vera had her own look, and Max had a charming way of remarking about her appearance. "You're a ten in my book, for sure," he'd say. "But hey, wait ... doesn't make sense, does it? All sixes doesn't add up to a ten. Right?"

If one were to take each feature of Vera and judge it on a scale from one to ten, well, Max was probably right. Tallish, thinnish, her mane of dark auburn hair squabbled with her pale complexion: each vying for a higher score than six. Her waspy nose (as in straight, thin, and little) was unremarkable, and her lips were thin, but because of their lovely rosebud shape could maybe pass as a seven. Yet all together, her mediocre features became one stunning ten. The math didn't add up. Max was right. Vera wasn't pretty. She was fascinating: divine in the way a horse can be so breathtakingly beautiful and alluring, pulling one in, to become more majestic the closer one comes.

"I *said*, where is a mirror? And we need to set up physical therapy as soon as possible. What happened to that nurse?" Sally snapped. "I've had it with you, Vera," and threw the scuffies to the floor. "Sourpuss attitude. So sad and sulking all the time."

Straining to lift his head, Warren barked to clear his throat of the thickening mucus.

"Sally ... my God ... I'm dying."

Sally appeared stricken. Blew a short sigh through her nose, tightly closed her eyes, and spoke with a renewed confidence. She corrected her dying father.

"Dad, I will not have you talking like this," she said.

"Sally!" Warren spat at her. "I am dying.... Dying ... you Goddamn fool."

CHAPTER 3

UNCLE

Wrong must not win by technicalities.

—Aeschylus, *The Eumenides*

ate morning. Warren's third day in the hospital resembled the day before. Awake here and there. A growing number of episodes that could pass as serious panic attacks.

Vera and Uncle Nelson stood face-to-face beside Warren's hospital bed.

Vera felt his fire.

"Who do you think you are, exactly?" he asked.

"Last time I checked, I was Warren's daughter."

"Who are you to decide who can come and go?"

"Didn't I just tell you who I am?"

"Ya. Well, I'm his brother," Nelson countered.

"You haven't seen Dad since Easter. It's almost Halloween."

"I'm family."

Her tired, unblinking eyes rested on Uncle Nelson's shadowy ones, and she suddenly found herself in a staring contest with him. She held steady and surmised his thoughts: bossy little bitch, as always … know it all, like her father. Nelson had aged, though, a charcoal smoldering now, with less burn, less strength.

"Where's Sally?" Nelson said and broke the stare.

She had a spark of mightiness. "Well … like I said, Dad made very clear to me he didn't want any visitors hovering around his bed at the end." Damn. He knows I'm lying. Dickhead.

"Are you listening, Vera? We're family."

With his bright, unblemished white sneakers planted about two feet from Warren's bedside, he craned his neck, "Hey, brother." Wiggled his hands in the pockets of his stretchy black sweatpants.

A nagging worry returned: maybe Warren could see everyone in the room from a vantage point on the ceiling. Jesus. This hypothesis had been somewhat supported by studies and accounts of people deemed officially dead who came back to life—she hoped they were all wrong. What does officially dead mean, anyway? Plus, there was no data from the dead who stayed dead. Yes, there was hope. Warren lay in bed and would stay there. He wasn't monitoring the room from above. Wasn't watching what she did.

She scanned Nelson's entourage—wife Alice and two adult children—and had a quick ping of self-assurance. Just do the right thing. For Warren. Warren.

Aunt Alice and Vera's cousins, Mark and Nancy, stood shoulder to shoulder, forming a three-headed shape of almost monstrous proportions. The six eyes stared at her. They all had the same frumpy, mismatched look: unassuming and nonthreatening, the way blue bloods like to surprise the unsuspecting person they're talking to with the sudden shock of just how ordinary they truly are. Only Nelson and Alice weren't blue bloods. And they weren't athletes either. They had all filed into the hospital room, glancing side to side as if looking for a stray soccer ball or idle lacrosse stick, when, in truth, watching television was always the sport of preference. They were all dressed in assorted colors of shiny, stretchy athletic attire covered with little balls of fabric from too many washings. Clumped together, they gave off a flowery odor of fabric softener.

"Hey, Warren. It's your brother here," Nelson croaked.

Warren nodded his head, opened his eyes, and closed them again. He'd had a nice sleeping spell. Nelson kept talking to him, question after question to which Warren didn't respond.

Vera sat down squarely in the middle of the green recliner and tried not to think. Had to look somewhere. She was running out of things to stare at. The taupe-painted wall behind the head of Warren's bed showcased various medical apparatuses, all in their proper place, like cubist art thoughtfully displayed: a lively and three-dimensional showing in metal and plastic. The coiled clear suction tube beamed readiness, the red plastic box politely asked for used needles, and the thick black cables were suspiciously silent. *My God. I need help. Seriously.* She drew in a large amount of air and exhaled, but it came out weak, a sad gush of uncomfortable sputtering. Her lungs were sore and tired.

Warren and Nelson were mismatched brothers. The adage about how opposites attract did not apply in this case; Warren and Nelson floated separately, in different directions—yin and yang lacking any interconnectedness.

Uncle Nelson had a predilection for disagreeing and argued endlessly with anybody about practically anything. After a lifetime of patience and compassion toward his disappointing only brother, why was it that her father should have his final hours disrupted by the likes of someone like Nelson? The same old Nelson who, standing at the bedside of his dying brother, would see and take (there was no doubt) the opportunity to finally emerge as the victor, the one with the final say. What remained of Warren was no match for the pull of this lifelong, wrenching conflict.

"Hey. Warr ..." Nelson said, brittle and too loud.

Warren broke into partial consciousness. It was frantic. Explosive and raw with feelings. His eyes were wide open with fear, his attempts to speak came out as unintelligible mumblings. What was it he was trying to say? What was it he needed?

Nelson backed away from the bed, headed to the corner, and burst into tears. Hung on to Alice. They all cried. Hung on to each other. Alice broke away, handed out tissues to everybody, and they shuffled about a bit to form a perfect line as if they were a team, and they gawked—in horror—at Warren's mumbling as he lay dying in bed.

Help me, God. Her eye caught the bedside monitor and its huge, attached steel arm, pulled out and bent at the elbow. The screen's constant flicker and beeping sound, now insignificant, brought to mind the red and blue flashing lights of a police cruiser after a murder, with people hanging around for no good reason. Hanging around for no good reason. Right.

Her father could die today, Vera felt it, and she was not going to allow any possibility whatsoever of having Uncle Nelson's puss in his face. She perked up.

"Shussss, Dad. It's okay." His lips frothed and she tried to stop his arms from flailing.

"Not a good time right now, Uncle Nelson," she heard herself say. This is when the dying really need you.

"I think his exact words were, 'Tell them I won't be taking any visitors now,'" and she straight-lined her lips to give the appearance of a sad smile.

From the corner, the mass sniffling stopped cold. She turned, singling out Nelson's dried eyes, and continued speaking with the calm confidence of a black-robed judge, delivering the verdict—the logical consequence—of not having what it took, whatever the reason, to be a loving brother to a brother who so wanted to love him.

"I can let you know when he's a little better, more awake for you, Uncle Nelson."

She continued, cracked her cemented smile, "Oh. And I'm sure he didn't mean you, Uncle Nelson ... his only brother ... when he said, 'No visitors,' must be so hard for Mark and Nancy to see" (considering they hardly know who he is, she wanted to screech) "... and you too, Aunt Alice. Must be hard for all of you." She was almost whispering now.

With his eyes closed, Warren appeared placid now, but his chest was heaving. He was working hard about something.

Nelson, cocking his head up unnaturally high, trumpeted, "That's what family's for," as the heads and eyes nodded at various tempos—too soon and for too long. "We'll come back another time. When he's better."

She read what Nelson meant by another time, a time without her there. But she was not leaving until Warren was good and dead.

"Good idea." She fixed another sad smile on her face and gazed downward.

They scurried out, eight legs at once.

A cool rush spread across her forehead. The nurse came into the room, and Vera watched her move about here and there. A windup toy came to mind, this thought petering out with a flash of just how disrespectful she could sometimes be.

The nurse left; Vera dragged her chair to the bedside. Placed her head on Warren's pillow, an anchor of flesh on flesh, and held him, covering him gently with a sail of winged arms. And Vera wept like never before.

CHAPTER 4

TRAVELERS

One does not get to know that one exists until one rediscovers

oneself in others.

—Goethe, Letter to Auguste Stolberg

arren's friend Martin was no Goddamn fool. This was con-firmed three hours after Uncle Nelson's visit.

Vera sniffed the air. The disinfectants had too much pine and not enough lemon, saturating room 350 with the heaviness of yet another unpleasant odor.

As Martin briskly walked into the room, he gave a quick squeeze to Vera's hand on his way to Warren's bedside. She had a nice feeling: relief, upon seeing her father's dear friend. With Martin here, all she had to do was sit and watch, no need for mon-itoring or facilitating small talk. She was no longer bothered by the room's distressing scent—as if it had suddenly exited the room.

"Warren. It's Marty."

Martin's voice stirred Warren to consciousness. He opened his eyes, grinned with cracked brown lips, and Vera witnessed the painful act of a dying man's fight for alertness.

She had a pop-up vision of two playful red foxes: gentle and kind but crafty when necessary. Was this Martin's final bedside visit with her father? How ridiculous. No one knows how long it takes to die. No one ever does.

At the bedside, Martin reached across his sickly friend's sunken chest, and, with one hand cradling Warren's elbow, he shook the limp hand with a slow and measured force. She was struck by Martin's power—a ferocious kind of strength—now taming and calming.

Was Martin a Buddhist? She surmised Martin had seen all this before. Dutifully and reverentially, he had rehearsed many times the hospital scene: directed and acted, critiqued, and rewrote many interpretations. And now, surrounded by the force of familiarity, he seemed at ease with the sight and feelings of the horror laid before him. Martin's eyes spoke, and his voice cast a light, fusing acceptance. The acceptance of death. The acceptance of deep sorrow. Martin wasn't there for himself.

Warren's head bobbed. Still smiling, he shook his hand up and down in Martin's guiding grasp. He let go. Tried to wipe the dribbling drool from his chin onto the shoulder of his hospital gown; he tried to clear the sticky phlegm from his throat; he coughed up sputum; he gargled, and his whisper came out coarse and slow-moving. But it didn't matter.

Their eyes locked.

"Marty, good to see you, old man."

"Hope you're getting good service here, Warren."

Warren was quiet. Worked hard to keep his head up, follow the conversation.

"Or do I need to make some waves here?" Martin winked.

They both smiled with tenderness, seemed almost happy.

"No, no, no … my friend. No waves. A dying man doesn't need much, Marty."

There was a long pause. The smiles faded. The eyes stayed locked.

"I'm going to miss you, buddy," Martin said.

Martin was one of her father's friends who had aged well. A fine octogenarian he was, covered where need be, in his out-of-style pressed pants and herringbone sports jacket. A paradox of sorts. His frame was rheumatic, small, and arched. The color of his eyes a sad, faded blue, and yet he projected with confidence that special insight that aging can sometimes give. Martin was old indeed, but now, having lived a life, his greatest strength, his power, hailed from wisdom.

She was suddenly reminded of the not-so-dazzling versions of old age—the ridiculous octogenarian doubles-tennis group that played before her group every Wednesday morning. "Yes, I hit the courts every week," she once overheard one of the wizened old men say. At the time, she thought of the word *puffery*. Yes, a bird. The little man had looked like a bird to her, one of the countless small, inconsequential ones, the ones always pecking and making noise, always trying to plump out their chests. His brain was shrinking, she had reminded herself. All those once healthy, bulging convo-lutions, now flattened and thinning, sparking moments (perhaps days or even weeks) of grandiose delusion. Give the guy a break. Give them all a break, for God's sake—the whole tennis team. But still, their geriatric matches were a sad sight for spectators: a flock in loose white garb—sagging, spindly-legged, and beady-eyed. She guessed their weekly match was meant to be their show of defiance to the ravages of old age, but to her, it simply challenged the laws of physics. She would overhear their talk, usually relating to doctor office visits and which primary care doctors provided the necessary insurance referrals to the specialists, and perpetual physical therapy. "A Goddamn miracle," Warren would have said if he had been forced to sit and watch a match. Vera smiled for the first time in many days.

Other cultures appreciated how to age well, more wisely, more gracefully than her American one. Didn't fight it as much. When younger, unmarried, in a perpetual manic phase, and crazed with the drive to succeed (Max had called it the Ayn Rand state of mind), she often passed such a finely aged group on the corner of Hanover and Prince Street in Boston's Italian North End. They were octogenarians from the old country of northern Italy. This, too, was a sporting team, with many players—but in a social sense—all gathered around a rusted metal table to sip, talk, and laugh. Share wisdoms. Warren and Martin could have had a seat at that table.

And she remembered one evening while having dinner on Prince Street. She and Max were dating then. Max had looked over at her through the candlelight, against a pressed white linen tablecloth and a petite crystal vase with pink primroses. She remembered feeling so beautiful, so blushing that night. "You know, my love," he had said, "those Italians. Yup. They're a special group. Have it right. I'd like a seat at their table. Their Mediterranean diet is not only healthy, with solid statistics for longevity to back it up, but quite palatable, as well." He loved to repeat a great lead-in when he found one, and she had wondered at the time if she was the first to have heard this one.

"Well, the Mediterranean encompasses a large region, you know, Max. Besides Italy you have Spain, Greece, parts of France, and they all have a variation of the Mediterranean diet." She had challenged him, as always (she knew he loved her for it).

"As with anything, my love, you take the best parts from the best places ... *il migliore in absoluto*!" And Max had laughed. "I intend to age well," he had said.

She missed this, the sound of his laugh and his attempts to speak in multiple languages, which he failed at miserably. Despite his linguistic mix-ups, Max had an Olympian air about him that contrasted charmingly with his unassuming conversational style. "I'm just a mutt," he'd say with the right crowd. Max would have aged well—if he'd had the chance.

Martin pulled up the orange plastic chair, placing it directly beside Warren's bed. Bending at the waist, he propped himself up with his elbow next to Warren's and kept it there. Kept it there.

Warren whispered, "We had some good times, Marty." Determined to plow through the thickening phlegm in his throat.

"... fishing trip in '84 ... Bugaboo Creek."

Martin's elbow remained next to Warren's, in an awkward position, "I still say the pilot of that floatplane was high ... on something," Martin said.

Warren's head dropped. It lay there, on his left shoulder.

Excruciating—the sadness she was witnessing. But she could

see this was all Warren wanted, needed from his dear friend. Acceptance, acknowledgment. A sharing of his sorrow.

Looking away and up, she removed herself from the surroundings and daydreamed. She imagined Martin take on the shape of a giant man: watched him weep at Warren's bedside and she could almost taste his salty tears. Heard him cry out for answers as to why his beloved Warren should die and leave him alone in this cold, jagged world of too few Warrens. And then suddenly, before her eyes, Martin shrank. He became tiny. Tiny enough for her to hold, so she cupped him in her hands and held him tightly against her beating chest, and together they wept at the sight of their beloved Warren.

Comfortable silences led to nowhere.

The final conversation between Warren and Martin was a quiet one.

"You're a good man, Marty," Warren said, and struggled, pressed down on the bedsheets with his elbows, pushed back his shoulders, tried to elevate his bobbing head.

Martin plucked a stray hand towel from the bed, rolled it up, and gently placed it under Warren's head, straightening it with both hands. Stood at the bedside.

"You're the better man, Warren."

Warren tried to wink at his beloved Martin. "You mean better *fisherman*."

His eyelids drooped, and his head cradled gently into the towel.

For the first time, Martin looked away from him.

There was a determined flow in the air; a light breeze seemed to pick Vera up and carry her directly into Warren and Martin's path. She became a part of their connection. All-knowing, she grasped the core of her father. With the glossy layers of his life now stripped and peeled away, she could see laid bare the budding seed of his life and how he grew this into completeness. She savored the sweetness, the fruit of it, and wanted more. Closed her eyes, prayed to God, thanked God, for she too had it—this core—like her father. Yes. She needed her own Martins to travel with, in her life and in her death. But who are they? My travelers.

CHAPTER 5

BIRDS & LADYBUGS

My master is the hard fact, how things are.

—Napoleon

Day four. Morning. Vera woke up in her bed, lay flat to gaze at the ceiling, and remembered Sally's words from the night before: "Seriously, Vera. Go home and sleep. Uncle Nelson won't be back when it's this late. Besides, you don't want to faint, do you? Like all the other times."

Vera hadn't wanted to leave Warren, and her gut wouldn't quiet down, seemed to roll round and round, saying, "He could die tonight." But she had gone home, and here she was, lying in bed looking up and wondering if he was already dead and she had missed it: being with him for his final breath. For him. For her.

She rose, pulled her unwashed hair into a thick ponytail and looked briefly at herself in the full-length mirror. Didn't care to linger today, on herself or her white silk pajamas. She blindly reached for her clothes, thrown over the stupidly huge club chair she could never recall sitting on. She pulled and yanked to fit into her dark navy jeans. No jewelry today. Adjusted her ponytail.

There was always a ponytail. High or low, slick or loose, depending on the event. "Works well for you, Vera. It's an invitation to look only at your face," Max had once disclosed, as if having discovered one of the great mysteries of the portrait painting world, and he was now sharing it with only her. Her best friend Sean had also alerted her regarding a summation of her whole look: "You know, My Miss Vera, you pull off a classic—almost regal—aura with le uniform of yours: dem designer jeans, T-shirt, and killer shoes. Expensive jewelry too, of course. Relatively speaking."

"T-shirt? When do I ever wear T-shirts," she had replied.

"Okay. I'm mixing you up with someone else. The almost-regal thing still holds, though," Sean had said.

She landed in her sleek kitchen, turned to the wireless speaker, and said, "Play Mahler, *Symphony No. 5, Adagietto.*"

This piece had been recommended to her by Sean. Need a Sean fix soon.

In an absurdly loud voice, Vera commanded, "Increase the volume."

She glanced at her coffeemaker. Was Dad still alive? They'd call, right?

She had been antsy for that first morning sip of sugary coffee. This was what got her up from staring at the ceiling above her bed. Grabbed her pre-programmed mug and collapsed on the stool in front of the black granite island. She could listen to this concerto piece endlessly, delighted with the sheer loudness of it all. Following the thread of melody through the blare, she kept herself squarely in the beauty of the moment and far away from Warren's bedside.

Vera swallowed. Max had been addicted too, and she tried to block any further association of her coffee with Max. Unsuccessfully. He liked it black, slightly cooled. Like her.

"Glad to be rid of him. Will always love him." This was the usual answer to anyone who asked her about Max, after they were divorced but before he died. To utter "Glad to be rid of him" after he died of a brain aneurysm would have been a bit harsh, so she replaced the sentence with "I'll miss him." Not that many asked. The second part of her response was the hardest for her to say, and every once in a while, she'd leave it out. But she knew deep down that she would always love Max. Was Max traveling with Warren as he slowly died? The already dead must travel too. Right. Guide the way or something.

She heard Sean tapping at the kitchen window. True traveler. Best buddy.

Vera shuffled to the locked door.

Sean entered with ease, made immediate eye contact, held a hand to his chest and paused. Stretching his arms around her, he took in a long breath, and they clutched each other. Briefly, but with force. She leaned away, and Sean headed to the island with a subtle version of his usual strut—his long legs looking cramped. He plopped a bakery bag down, sat, and patted the stool next to him.

"How we doing?"

Sean brushed back his thin, honey-colored, chin-length hair. Uncovered half his face. His low side part made for this necessary, repeated motion, which usually ended with his face cocked upward, giving the illusion that his nose was in the air.

"Doing."

"You look great."

"What?"

"The fitted white linen shirt, red flat ballet shoes."

"Why are you so focused on how people look? Really annoying," Vera said, and hunched over her coffee.

"Maybe because I'm so good-looking and I want people to prioritize looking good."

"How perfectly teeny-weeny minded of you. Not in the mood for this, Sean. Don't care what I look like right now. Maybe never will," she said. Her tone initially confrontational but sad by the last word.

"Whatever you need. I'm here, okay, Vera? It's always so hard to read you."

"What?"

"You have sort of a non-expressive face. Not stone-like, but you don't gesture much, I guess."

"What? Maybe because I'm *listening* to you," she said. "What would you like to see me do, Sean? Change my facial expressions all the time like a clown? Nod my head, wring my hands? Run my fingers through my hair to tip you off that I'm frustrated? We've evolved to the point where we have language, Sean. Words to express ourselves. Not grunts and gestures."

"Well. Like I said. It's hard to know what you're thinking."

"I'll tell you whatever I'm thinking, when I want you to know what I'm thinking."

"Well, it does come off as dignified and polished, I suppose. Like Queen Elizabeth or something. Anyway," he said, "thought I'd drop off some breakfast stuff. English muffins, your favorite marmalade. As you know, I'm not the tuna and green bean casserole type. Where's your toaster?"

Stop taking this out on Sean.

They sat at the island, drank coffee, and ate.

"This mug is hilarious," Sean said. "Know Your Tapeworms. This little yellow one has a kind of friendly, happy face. We eat way too much sushi, you know."

"Hey. Let's just sit together and not talk. I want you here with me, Sean. I love you. I just don't feel like talking."

"Got it."

True to form, Vera thought about Max. The thought of his calm steadiness jogged her memory. She knew what calm and steady looked like. Lived with it for twenty years. She pretended to feel it—a fraudulent totally together person—and her breathing slowed, she felt centered, kind, and good. Or something close to it.

She and Max had met at a party in Boston. It could have gone either way. Vera was single, thirty-one years old, and on the prowl for a guy with some measure of intellect. Number one criterion.

"You live round here? How'd you get invited to the par-tay?" Max had smiled.

"Ya. Around the corner. Old college friend of mine is our host."

"That so?"

"Ya. Gretchen is great. We met junior year. One of those friends you keep in touch with ... you know?"

"That so." Max nodded.

"Ya. That so," she fired back.

"Huh. Don't know her."

"That so."

"That so."

"You know I get the distinct feeling that as you perseverate, you're also scanning the crowd."

"That so." Max had smiled and looked at her from the corners of his eyes.

"I'm impressed. You can do two very taxing things at the same time."

"That so." And he smirked (or was it his version of a smile), looking her directly in the eyes.

"Seriously," she said flatly. "You keep on perseverating and scanning. I'm getting another drink."

She remembered being highly disappointed with Max at first. Seemed like a dumbass, looking for some sex, hoping she was a dumbass too. But she was wrong.

Got her drink and for the next hour found herself scanning the party crowd. For Max. She watched him navigate with ease, entering and exiting small bubbles of people. From a distance, he had a cocky walk. Vera could see he continued with the small talk, eyes roaming. When Max finally made it back to her solitary bubble, he learned all about her and she learned all about him, with Max not once uttering "that so" or taking both his eyes off her. Max was from Connecticut (Wilton); absolutely loved living in Boston (the vibe of it, with all the colleges and students); viewed Boston as a gritty city in some respects, but a smart city (a treasure trove of great art museums, music performances); and planned to stay for a while (looking forward to some skiing and hiking outside the city). Psychologist. Hospital-based practice.

Single and seriously funny. He dramatized hilarious stories about some of his nameless crazy patients (it wasn't until five years later that Congress passed healthcare privacy regulations). He laughed about being a "trust fund free" poor kid from Connecticut. "A lot of pressure, to be sure, inheriting so much money, don't you think?" he had asked, waiting for her to answer. The guy was no dummy. And she could sense he was attracted to her. Max was smart, funny, super masculine. A Russell Crowe from *Gladiator*. Max couldn't sing, though. Torturous to hear him sing even "Happy Birthday." She felt lucky to have found Max. Lucky to know true love. Lucky, lucky, lucky. Untouchable when it came to tragedy and deep sorrow then.

After over twenty years of a good marriage (better than good), she still occasionally pondered the question of why they divorced. Almost two years out now, Vera summed it all up in one word: sex. He wanted more of it, she didn't.

And so, the story goes. Or went. The insidious breakup of a good marriage, mainly because of the great societal illusion that all women should want to have crazy sex forever and ever, until their last breath.

Half an hour went by, and Sean spooned another glob of marmalade onto his plate. She took another bite of her limp English muffin. Doesn't he know what toasted means? These aren't toasted. Just warmed up.

Stop it. This frustration. Max. The past. For the love of God!

"I'm so sorry this is happening to you, Vera." Sean said. His voice cracking, his eyes watery.

The best she could give back was a vacant stare.

The caller ID blinked. A thickening spread upward in her throat—she tried to swallow it without success. Jesus. Can they say … in a telephone message? If someone …

She pressed playback: "Please call the hospital nurses' station on floor three. It is now 10:00 a.m. You may want to come to the hospital now." They left a phone number.

Sean's long, lean arms blanketed and held her there for a while. She was struck with an urge to cry—was on the verge—like on the verge of needing to sneeze or cough. But like some, without reason, her urge died. She felt comforted by Sean's silence and low-key demeanor. After a while, he let himself out.

She sat down at the island. Her eyelids gently shuttered, soothing her with a soft curtain of black silence and protection. She raised them and looked out the large window, resting her gaze on the expanse of lush green lawn and fading flower garden. The shock of acknowledging such beauty made her feel tiny and vulnerable, like a bird or ladybug. She liked this sometimes: when she pretended to be so little, so inconsequential in the presence of nature's power, she couldn't possibly have anything at all to do with her future or fate. It's all out of my hands. So ridiculously obvious. One unexpected frost and poof—I'm dead.

But she could never stay in this state of mind for long; wished she could, but she had to accept it. Particular ladybugs and birds instinctively sensed a change in the weather and sought shelter and life. The others, those who refused to act, met a frigid death.

Her mug was empty. Max was dead, her father was dying, and she was very much alive, alone and merely looking out on a fading fall garden: created by a well-known landscape designer and maintained by a well-paid gardener. And yes, it would be okay, would be fine, much easier, for her to look up and surround herself with the green lushness of life in a romantic, optimistic way. Simply deny the understanding of what she had witnessed between her dying father and his friend Martin, deny the ways in which she could right now alter her life somehow, to make it more meaningful and satisfying, her death perhaps a little less difficult. Hey. Just let destiny lead the way. This would be nice and easy. But, instinctively, Vera's need was to do the opposite.

She pressed playback: "Please call the hospital nurses' station ..."

CHAPTER 6

CHOICE

It is hard to fight an enemy who has outposts in your head.

—Sally Kempton, "Cutting Loose"

After Sean left, Vera called the nurses' station and was informed Warren appeared to have taken a turn for the worse.

The car seemed to pilot on automatic as it whizzed past all the familiar sights. From the click of her seatbelt to where she was now, standing in the hospital's main lobby, Vera could not remember much of the drive.

The arena-sized lobby was newly polished, shone harsh and glassy. She heard the whining of a buffer machine, and from the corners of her eyes saw a janitor whirling the machine in small concentric circles. She looked up. Was surprised by the mighty array of fluorescent bulbs over her head, the drone of their busy humming—and she felt exposed, bathed in the sad shallowness of their artificial glow. She was slightly sweaty, dreamy too, as if slightly sedated—unsure of her whereabouts. In the center of all this glare and brilliant light, she stood silent, her mind battling to focus on the task at hand. Walk to his room. Do not faint.

Her heart pounding, she felt the onset of that familiar, black, icy terror. Tried to push it away, but she couldn't. She tried to manage the suddenly heightened awareness of all her senses: quell their dangerous exaggeration. Fought hard to spawn a state of generalized numbness. Feeling fine. Right. But she wasn't fine.

It was as if she had been transported in a giant bubble from the hospital parking garage to the center of this massive columned lobby for the sole purpose of silent observation. As if slapped with a clipboard, her clear mission was to observe and record the busy rushing about of green scrubs and white coats, pink aprons, hair nets and foot scuffies, each en route to accomplish the important duties of the day.

Jesus. What shape will he be in?

How she had landed in this crowded, glass-enclosed, cavernous lobby was a patchwork of memory, a madras of color mixed with action and still life. Irregularly shaped pieces once scattered, Vera connected them, as if stitching from a grand design. Her design. Warren had once said: "A person's memory is just their grand design." Or was it Sean who had said this? Maybe Max. Just don't faint.

She looked for a pattern, a beginning or an end. Briefly, she imagined the checkered hues of blue—her blue parked car. She held on to this piece, the color blue, and found it soothing, with all the people traffic moving about her on the polished hospital floor, intent on avoiding a jam here or a collision there.

Vera. Pull it together. Dear God. Don't let me faint.

Standing in the lobby, feeling too small to be noticed, she paused. Thought about her blue car again: her force, her polished cobalt BMW, her enameled carriage of brutal recklessness (should she so choose). She felt the beginnings of dizziness. There is a choice here. Dumbass.

But she was still panicky. Her chest throbbed, her breathing was rapid and shallow. She couldn't catch her breath. Her thoughts suddenly went rogue, carried her away, and she remembered the steep climb of her car up the parking garage. It had been monumental, Babylonian in nature. A tower of rounded concrete curves, tight and low, winding ancient and ceremonial, as if to one day be recounted as a legendary event—a procession turned suddenly swift and wild into the fast lane—a fearless chariot driver commanding and harnessing the great strength of muscle and a flowing mane. The energy felt unstoppable. She could see herself drive it hard and wild until the very end, until her tires were met with the force of friction, of rubber against concrete. She heard the imagined screeching of car breaks, and it jolted her. She searched and found her legs, wooden and immobile.

The dizziness was stubborn. Trying to take her down. She hit back hard: kept her head perfectly still, stopped the perceived motion with the greater and opposite force. Her legs signaled movement—the push against the floor and the floor pushing back against her. She was moving.

Above, large bold letters spelled out patient floors in bright red. Her legs stopped, she stood beneath the signage. Slowly stretching her neck, she pulled the rubbery skin from lax to taut. Felt her chin, flesh covered, yet bone hard, change location—up and to the right—ending with a slight tilt of her head that she held in an exaggerated position as if to savor this great knowledge of having just successfully moved her head without fainting. Damn.

And it happened, unexpectedly—a surge of relief: a radiant wakefulness, a newborn clarity, a divine wholeness. She, Vera Mine, possessed a net force, both mighty and powerful: an internal force, a self who could and would propel her stiff inert legs into motion and keep her walking.

I'm fine.

The overhead signage beckoned and surprised as she made her way to room 350. Each turn, each corner offering a choice—vibrantly displayed in neon-colored words with contrasting arrows—each selection leading to the next possibility, the next destination.

The word maternity kept popping up, teasing her, and she found herself searching for it. The maternity letters were in canary yellow with big purple arrows (so cheery). She would rather follow this route: see all the new babies lined up in rows behind sparkling glass and catch a glimpse of one or two of them in the arms of a giddy mother or father, standing so proud and official-like, witnesses to that first vital cry of a healthy son or daughter. She would like to see those flushed, happy faces—surround herself with relief, that pure elation of a birthing finally over, a birthing without complication, without any nasty surprises.

She could meander about holding a colorful bouquet of flowers, pretend to be on her way to visit someone special. Smile at everyone—and they would smile back at her. Nice. A noisy place, of hushed laughter and sweet cries—a place full of life. But she needed to follow the signs in bright red with the white arrows, the signs reading patient floors—the signs leading her to unsmiling hallways, to the hushed wards, to the lineup of rooms holding back the patients who silently sweltered in their beds. She kept going. One step in front of another. How will he be?

The countdown. Room numbers were cropping up. Messing with her head. 340, 341, 342. The room numbers were black and unusually large, their giant size almost comical in nature, standing ready, at attention, to assist.

The huge numbers spoke to Vera, at first in a whisper. They told her their story: of the hospital personnel's lengthy deliberations over their size (should they be four inches high or five or five and a half?); of the many focus groups about them (they were so flattered); of the latest in architectural design and wayfinding. The final consensus—expensive, custom-made, colossal sized six-inch numbers, to be screwed onto blue eggshell pastel walls exactly thirty-two-and-a-half inches from the floor (the height deliberation having been one of the livelier and more heated discussions, the numbers recount). The numbers laughed. "Our size is ridiculous," they snickered. "We're absurd."

Picking up her pace, she was at a hasty clip. But the numbers, too, sped up; they spoke faster, spoke louder. They bellowed, roared, screeched at her. Stop, Vera!

She kept walking.

Suddenly, the numbers were briefly serene, leaned toward her, swaying: appealed to her humbly and modestly—gently asked her to stop, to please listen, to pause for a moment and rest, yes, rest—hear the sad personal stories of those held behind the swollen wooden doors. "You must, Vera. How could you not? *We* won't let you faint," the numbers cooed.

But the numbers' strength was not enough—their frightful echo, their heated intensity, their searing commands. They were too weak against the blistering will of Vera Mine. She saw it, number 350. The oversized door was ajar. She pushed the thick, heavy door wide open.

His eyes were open, and he smiled faintly at her. She faltered into the room and stood.

CHAPTER 7

DR. COOKE

It is not so much the suffering as the senselessness of it
that is unendurable.

—Friedrich Nietzsche

Day Five. Room 350. Warren slept most of the time now, his mouth wide open. He had intense episodes several times an hour in which he seemed to be struggling into a state of partial consciousness.

"What do you mean?" Sally said, standing in the overly lit room, her shadow reflected on the hospital window against the dark night outside.

Room 350 felt like a sauna. And both she and Sally had been sitting in it for the last ten hours. Vera was clammy all over. She had never cared for a sauna's intense heat: the edges of her nostrils burning, the temperature rising, the oozing sweat, the continual question of endurance—stay a few more seconds or escape. Absent here, of course, was any possibility of a lakeside plunge into ice cold water.

"I mean ... you were there on the first day Dad was admitted. When the nurse gave him his pills. Right?" Vera asked.

She glanced at Sally's yellow chrysanthemums—no longer so pretty and perky. Beginning to fade and arch over. Fresh water and newly cut stems might help them. Maybe not. Maybe too late.

"It was Nora, right?" Sally sniffed the flowers and moved them an inch to the left. "They need more sunlight," she said.

"I think Nora is Dad's nurse again tonight," Vera said faintly.

"Oh?" Sally said, and slowly turned toward her.

Vera fidgeted with her plastic car key. Her underarms were sticky. Sally really was trying. In her own way. Right. Right.

"Nora could be the one on … when he dies," said Vera.

Sally strode to the green recliner, sat, crossed her legs, examined her calves.

"What about it …"

"When he dies."

"And I suppose *you* know when this will be," Sally said sharply and touched her long bangs. Pushed blond strands of hair to one side. "What's your point, Vera?"

"I don't know."

"One of the nurses asked if we wanted hospice, the other day," Sally said.

"And?"

"I didn't know. Said I would talk with you first."

Vera let out a slow sigh, sensed that familiar creeping sadness of solitude. It was the worst kind. Complete loneliness while in the company of an intimately known human being. It sucked. Everything sucked. Jesus.

She thought back to a few days before, during one of Warren's better spells. Nurse Nora had shown up: softly rounded yet rigid, carrying a small paper cup of Warren's pill packets.

"Well, hello," Warren had greeted her with a wheeze. And obvious effort.

"I'm Nora," she had said flatly, not looking at him.

Silence.

"And what miracle pills might you have for me today?" Warren had asked, as he tried to pep himself up, hold on to a bit of what he once was—make it clear that he wasn't dead quite yet.

Silence.

"Is this enough juice to take these pills? Do you need more?"

"Oh, should be fine."

And with what plainly looked to Vera like a forced grin, Nurse Nora focused on the opening of pill packets. Warren had taken on a slightly hurt expression.

"Didn't you get the sense Nora wasn't very invested with, you know … helping Dad …"

"Helping Dad what? Gave him his pills on time. What else is the nurse supposed to do?"

"I don't know … try to give him more than just pills." Vera pursed her lips to one side.

Sitting upright in the recliner, Sally looked at her hands, spread her fingers out wide.

"There was an edge of contempt in Nora's voice," said Vera. "She doesn't even try to hide it."

"You know, Vera," Sally said, "we don't know what's going to happen with Dad. You can't take it out on the nurse. Nobody knows what's next. Like this Nora has a crystal ball or something.

She was having a bad day. Never happens to you, I suppose." Sally lay back on the recliner, extended it with unnecessary force. Vera found herself lost in Sally's blank stare for a few seconds. She emerged to hear herself encouraging Sally to go home and get some sleep. Whispered, "I'll keep you posted."

"Okay," Sally mumbled, her face ruddy and eyes hooded. She stood, her yoga jacket tied around her waist. "Wow. Dark already. Call me when anything happens. I hope he isn't too uncomfortable. I cry myself to sleep every night. You know. I hope all his scary episodes stop."

They rarely hugged each other, so it was a gangly, awkward affair, lacking sincerity. Neither one seemed to notice. Nor care. Sally walked out the door with less strut than usual.

Vera had seen the Nurse Nora type before. Everywhere, really. Some might consider Nora a good nurse: if one were to look at her attendance record, note-keeping, ass-kissing to the right people, and the absence of patient-related complaints (what would the complaint be? I'd like to report someone from the reptile family posing as a *Homo sapiens*), an argument could, in fact, be made for the promotion of Nurse Nora based on merit. Nurse Nora signed up for all the advanced training: seminars, conferences, retreats.

The head of the hospital bed was at a thirty-degree angle. Warren was too weak against the force of gravity to hold his head up now; he was swollen, his skin sticky and slimy. His better state yesterday seemed a long time ago. Mostly he slept—a heaving mass in fetal position. Hibernating and waiting, as those around him waited, as the world waited, for him to be taken. Without warning, his panicked consciousness would break through— feverishly begging to her, thrashing, mumbling pleas for help. "Ma ... ma ... mama." With one sudden blink, a surge transformed into agitated gibberish. Babbling, his head jerking about, the pupils of his hollowed eyes rolling upward, leaving behind only the white. Frightful to witness. And was *he* frightened? The episodes were coming more frequently and with more intensity. Warren's last injection of morphine had been administered by Nurse Nora three or four hours ago.

Oh my God. He's going to die on Nora's shift. Jesus. Please, dear God, don't let this happen. My God.

She sat on the orange plastic chair, shoved up against the hospital bed, and found she could sit and lean the top half of her body on him, hold him with her head next to his head on the pillow. It helped to calm Warren during his fretful episodes. Helped him. Her.

With soothing words, she whispered, telling him to go to sleep. But he would not.

"It's okay to sleep, Dad."

"Close your eyes, Dad."

"Everything's okay, Dad."

"I'm here."

He wasn't dying in peace. Brain out of sync with body, the dark rhythm of his life seemed to plod on and on, a driverless carriage without destination: a feisty body, gone rogue. Jesus. He doesn't deserve this. This kind of ending.

Nora emerged, and Vera silently cursed. Damn. She was afraid of how it would go down. Was suddenly broken. The aggressive energy she'd had with cretin Uncle Nelson that had seemed so

just, was gone. She was weary—from all the begging to Nurse
Nora's pinched lizard eyes—and ashamed of her whoring, with all
the necessary facades of eternal sweetness and surrender. When?
When will this be over?

Nurse Nora loomed in the center of the doorway, her poise
suggesting power, authority. And Vera was suddenly cognizant of
the strength it would take for her to suppress the fiery effect Nora's
actions had on her. For Warren. For Warren.

Lifting her head from his pillow, trying to control her face,
she heard herself talking: the words spurting out deformed somehow, drawn out and stilted.

"So sorry to bother you, but Dad seems to be waking up since
the last morphine injection you gave him."

"Yes."

"Is there anything we … you … can do?"

Nora's face cemented into indifference, her smile unnaturally
precise and still.

"It's horrible … so horrible … to see him agitated and panic-
stricken like this …"

"Yes. It is."

Warren moaned. And Vera was hammered with a grim realization. It was happening. The luck of the draw would have her
brokering Warren's death with the diligent, hollow Nurse Nora.

"Yes … it's hard," Nora said, tonelessly. Scratched her ear,
slowly nodded her head up and down, focused on the bed railing.

Vera was silent. But it doesn't have to be hard, you ass. You
know so much! Help him go in peace. Let my father die as he
should. Don't let him suffer.

"Nora, do you think it might be time for another injection? Do you think you could do this for him? He looks so uncomfortable ...." And she scolded herself because the words tumbling out of her mouth might not have sounded nice enough.

Warren was feverish, swelling up more and more—she glanced at the empty catheter bag. Did he feel as bad as he looked? She didn't know. But Nurse Nora knew. This bitch knew.

"If you are asking me for another morphine injection, I would need to get an order from the doctor. And it will take some time," Nora said blandly, as if informing a fast-food customer that the special order of a burger without ketchup would take a little longer.

And just like that, Vera understood what was playing out before her. It was yet another painful realization: She was entirely on her own, didn't even know what she wanted. What should she lobby for? What were the options?

She stood up from Warren's bedside, shoved the plastic chair backward. Talked boldly to herself. I will get more morphine for my father. I will not allow him to have a pointlessly drawn-out and miserable death. Turning her head to face Nora, she said coolly, "I would like to talk with a doctor, please. As soon as possible." She flattened her lips, sporadically clenched her teeth.

"Well, as I said. Will take some time," Nora said. "And we don't want to give him too much morphine."

"What?"

"I can't be held responsible for him dying," Nora said.

And there it was—the truth revealed. Vera felt the explosive shock of anger. She was pissed.

"Which it is for you then?" Vera said, barely controlling the loudness of her voice.

"Excuse me?"

"Control freak?" Vera said, trying in vain to mimic Nora's affectation of not giving a shit. But Vera *did* give a big shit about all this.

Her anger led to mockery. With crazed sarcasm, Vera tried to provoke Nora as best she could. "Awwwww, let me guess, some kind of a religious freak? Doing God's work? Afraid the holy God will be mad at you for interfering with the holy plan. You know … the let-them-suffer part. Totally understandable. Keep him alive to suffer along … long enough so that he dies on the next shift, when you're not here. So hard. Poor you." Vera set her lips in a tightly slitted smile.

Seemingly unaffected, Nurse Nora stared, for once directly at Vera.

Vera decided to go with the facts.

"My father is dying with needless suffering—right now. I would like to speak with a doctor—right now, Nora. Thank you. And if you are not able to get in touch with a doctor right now—then I will find someone who can." She was firm and measured. Certain. As if in slow motion, Vera twisted her head around to look back at her father. She could be a warrior. Damn right.

"If I can. I'll get the medical intern Dr. Cooke," Nora said, a bit red-faced, yet appearing unmoved, despite Vera's rant.

Nurse Nora lumbered away with what Vera thought was a snarl of a smile.

During the next five minutes, the worry crept in. Am I imagining things? Was that a snarl? Vera developed significant doubt about what she had just said and done. This compounded with her returning horror of fainting—she'd be unable, then, to do anything at all. Had she been too harsh with Nora? Had the bitch cursed her and marched off to a coffee break? A frenzy of heat rushed up inside of her, clouded with dapples of shadowy gray. Always the doubt. She held on to the bed rail. Focused on it. Should I put the bed rail up? Lower it? Right. Is Warren watching all this from above? Right.

A slight young man appeared wearing a hip-length white coat and a stethoscope wrapped around his neck. The coat and the stethoscope looked too big for him. He paused, cautiously stepped to the opposite side of the bed. With one glance, she could see he was not familiar with this dying thing, but he didn't seem afraid of it. Couldn't remember how, but her head was back on Warren's pillow, her lips and nose against his cheek, the warm wetness reassuring her.

"Is he having breakthrough episodes of consciousness? Difficulty breathing?"

Vera raised her head, politely stood up. "When he looks like he's having a panic attack?"

"I'm so sorry. I haven't introduced myself. Dr. Cooke. I'm a first-year intern," he said, his voice shaky. "And you are Ms. Mine?"

"Yes. My father, Warren."

Warren started another episode.

"Well ... Dr. Cooke ... the nurse gives him an injection of morphine every now and then, and at first he sleeps, but he's doing this more and more now. He seems frightened. Is he?"

Not waiting for an answer, Vera blurted out, "He needs more morphine to die right."

She panicked. Oh, God. Oh Jesus! Should I have said …

He looked so young: too young. Yet another worry: an inexperienced doctor now in charge of Warren's death. She didn't want to go over his head, but she would if she had to. Damn right.

She reacted to the contrast of a cropped cotton coat of white against skin so smooth, deepest black—and it jarred her. Slightly dizzy, she locked on to his eyes. And there, in the concentric reflections in the eyes of Dr. Cooke, she could see herself next to Warren. The vision was comforting: a diffuse caramel rooted within the warm brown of his speckled irises.

And as the luck of death would have it, the young intern led the way. They were a team now. Dr. Cooke, Vera, and her dying father.

The now energetic and enthusiastic Nora hopped to it. Nurse Nora set up a continuous morphine drip.

Dr. Cooke stayed. "Have you seen hospice?"

Vera shook her head.

"Well, keep in mind that your father's senses are heightened now," he said. "Dim the lights, don't repeatedly touch him all over. The last thing to go is probably his hearing, so keep this in mind. Look for frowning. This could mean he needs more medication. Morphine. If the mucus builds up too much, I can order atropine to dry it up. I'll drop in now and then. Let me know if you have any questions. If I can help in any way."

Vera nodded.

She switched off the lights. Turned on the flashlight of her cell phone. Didn't caress him. Was on guard for frowning.

Death can take a long time. Slowly, body organs shut down, a domino effect, each fallen piece taking out the next. But in what order, and how long would it take? It was difficult to watch at first. I can do this … it's almost over. Warren succumbed to a deep, undisturbed sleep: gone were the sudden semiconscious episodes filled with wailing and thrashing. She thought each slow, labored breath he was able to finish might be his last. But it never was. It went on and on, this waiting for death, and she experienced a new kind of tiredness: on watch for the death of the dying. It was one in the morning.

Dr. Cooke regularly checked in with offers to help in any way. Stood around for a while, searching within her eyes and acknowledging to Vera, "Yes, this is happening, and it really sucks." Nurse Nora popped in every now and then to ask if Vera needed anything, without the acknowledgment of how much it all sucked.

One of Vera's lurking nightmares had to do with being buried alive by mistake: waking up from a deep sleep or coma with her nose an inch away from the inside lid of a closed coffin, staring up at a white satin puffy pillow—buried impossibly deep in the ground. She occasionally caught an image of the unspeakable thought while watching a movie preview or reading an excerpt from a book or poem. It was one of those visions where she had to turn the page or cover her eyes, block the thought. She would make sure this didn't happen with Warren. The one thing he'd told her he wanted: cremation. And there was something else for her to do: thank Dr. Cooke on Warren's behalf.

So, she waited. And watched Warren slowly die. Clips from

those final hours would stay with her forever: the swelling and sweating, the unusual smell, the terrifying roller-coaster of agonal breathing. The troubling visions would never fully fade. Yet there was a maudlin gratefulness. A contentment of sorts from the sight of him in comfort. He was in a deep, deep sleep now. No longer any sudden, breakthrough panic attacks. And it was only then—watching Warren die well—that she was able to look beyond the physiology of his death, the grotesque mechanics of it all. Sitting next to him, she lightly held his withered hand and accepted his tortured and abused body: the continuous bubbling up of fluids closing off his throat and the halting, irregular, incomplete gasps.

Gently stroking his hand, she sensed he had taken her with him, with the others—his greatest accomplishments. His travelers. The aspect of eternity helped. Also, she would always know, always, that she had helped him die. For Warren. For Warren. A stirring of self-discovery overshadowed her fatigue.

And finally, with a babble of drowning in gurgling fluids, the breath came and went. It was the final one. There was no doubt. He was gone.

CHAPTER 8

REWORK A LIFE

Lying is done with words, and also with silence.

—Adrienne Rich, "Women and Honor:
Some Notes on Lying"

Two days before the funeral and Vera was drained. The incredible power and the extraordinary courage she'd had in the final hours of Warren's death were all gone.

"Every person has regrets," Warren had once told her. "To live is to have regrets."

A few regrets would sometimes pop up here and there, but they had more to do with inactivity on her part as opposed to doing something: standing mute while a bully pushed a nice kid around, not reporting to somebody (anybody) about the terrified looking little girl with heavy makeup and dressed like a prostitute being led around the mall by a creepy-looking guy, or driving by the chained dog shivering under a car in freezing weather. Always in too much of a hurry—something to do. And she was about to do it all over again. A regret because of her inaction.

Sally had taken care of the cremation.

Sally, Nelson, and Vera sat in the living room of Sally's condo. Uncle Nelson was sunk into the white linen couch, popping buttered popcorn into his mouth, one by one. She could see Sally was re-energized about something. She watched Sally's leather loafers—the pacing, and could see and hear the click of heels against the shine and resilience of the hardwood floors.

Everything in the room seemed cream colored, except for the chair she sat on. It was in the corner, an antique chair with a thinning red velvet cushion, hard and uncomfortable by nature. She tried to appear at ease. A trace of Korean stir-fry lingered in the air from the night before.

"Is it possible to highlight certain words within the write-up?" Sally yanked the cell phone away from her sweaty cheek and switched it to the other. Didn't put it on speakerphone. "Well, by highlight, I mean in bold print ... no, not italicized."

Vera was concerned about the obituary, this much she knew. Uncrossed her legs. Crossed them again. Sat up straight. Sally and Nelson seemed so contented. Odd. As if a monumental event was over, or something. With a nasty stab in her stomach, she surmised what the event had been. Sally and Nelson had put their keen literary skills to work on Warren's obituary: for them merely a long list of impressive accomplishments, cut and pasted into an agreed-upon configuration. A big job, this.

She leaned and arched her back forward, placed her elbows on her knees. Propped her head up with both fists. The rest of the day didn't look good for her. A swell of nausea came and went— thoughts of escape.

"What specific words? Oh ... well, chairperson, board member

... and his alma mater. Of course." Sally looked only at Nelson and rolled her eyes. Switched the cell again. Both cheeks were roughed up now.

Spurred on by Nelson's blank look as he sank deeper into the puffy couch, Sally raised her voice, "Bold print ... B-O-L-D ... so much easier for people to ... can they be capitalized ... at least?"

Sally halted her march. Locked her knees and sniffed.

"And to whom do I speak for something beyond the typical obituary ... for my poor dear father?" Sally tenderly half blew her nose with a tissue, said sweetly, "I've noticed you choose one per day, to highlight ... and place at the top of the page? Like Obituary-of-the-Day or something."

Nelson sped up his popcorn intake.

Vera could see Sally was now clearly pissed.

"Do I need to speak with someone else about this matter?" Crossed her eyes at Nelson and made the crazy sign, circling her finger at the side of her head. He looked clueless.

"Could I speak with one of your *senior* obituary writers?"

"Oh ... well, how is it you decide which obituary to headline?"

And on and on it went.

Sitting on the hard chair, Vera felt sorry for herself. She should be voicing a concern here and there; should be more forceful, more direct in taking on the self-appointed funeral organizers, Sally (mostly) and Nelson. But she couldn't seem to do it; couldn't seem to muster up the energy to speak on behalf of her dead father. She was a genuinely wretched person.

Her energy was zapped, and she couldn't do anything beyond listening and sleeping a lot. Everything around her shouted,

I am a triviality. The silly, grand illusion of herself as a warrior—
armed with shield and spear—had died with Warren. She'd had no
control over Warren's death, really. The mere serendipity of a hospital staffing calendar, Dr. Cooke and morphine had determined the
course of Warren's death—had saved the day—not she.

Such hubris, for her to have ever thought that she alone could
have affected the course of her father's death: such outrageous
arrogance. She thought she had been prepared for his death;
Warren wouldn't live forever. And yes, she had, during her short-
lived Buddhist phase, visualized Warren as dead. And yes, so
naive as to envision him vanishing from her life and leaving her
with lovely memories—after closing his eyes for the nighty night
of death—without anguish, without agony, without any need for
morphine. It was doing a job on her: coming to terms with the terrifying yet true images she now had as they replaced the false ones.

Sometimes, when her demonizing thoughts needed to be countered, Dr. Cooke's eyes would come into view. This simple memory
of looking into the young intern's brown speckled eyes softened
Vera with deep hope, love, and belief in the caring gentleness of
people. She hoped his eyeballs would stick around with her forever.

"Vera, hey there. Yoo-hoooo ... would you like to read the nice
obit for Dad? Nelson and I worked so hard on it."

The length of the obituary alone was plain silly, with such
a long list of deeds, it took up nearly three columns. It appeared
as if Warren had been a part of every organization known to man,
with the appropriate superlatives, including magna cum laude this,
Phi Beta Kappa that, chairman of this, member of that, Master
Mason. He was without equal, larger than life.

She couldn't remember Warren being chairperson of the town council for six years; he had been a board member for only two and quit. She remembered this because he had complained to her about it once. "I don't believe I have ever seen such a group of misfits all sitting around one table at the same time," he had said.

Barely giving her enough time to read it, Sally trilled, "Don't you like it? I didn't know Nelson remembered so many things about Dad that I didn't! Things you probably didn't even know about Dad ... anyway ... I think Dad would have liked it." And Sally elongated her neck, blinking. Paused to examine one of her fingernails up close. Glossy pazzazle pink today.

Vera hadn't spoken out loud to anyone for a long time, wasn't sure the words would come together as they should and tried hard not to sound meek.

"Ah ... so ... what's ... in Dad's obit ..."

Nelson stopped chewing, his cheeks bulging.

"Dad never graduated from college, and you know it," Vera said with surprising punch.

"Oh. What ... I'm sure Dad must have. You know ... with the G.I. Bill and all ... he never bragged about himself. You know...."

Nelson sucked the salt and butter from one of his fingers, and Sally faintly hummed and said, "Well, if he didn't ... he almost did, and that's good enough for me...."

Vera's tongue felt swollen and heavy, in the way of her words. "Do you know ... what ... a lie ... is?"

"My, my, my, Vera. Relax. It's not a lie ... I remember Dad telling me he graduated ... with honors, by the way."

"Bullshit."

"Vera. There will be a chance for you to write something nice about Dad on the funeral home's website. Would be nice to have a lot of comments. You can submit them anonymously. You know."

Vera had stopped listening. Had an inclination to cover both her ears—curl into a ball and roll unassumingly out the door. Was suddenly angry because the chair she sat on was so hard.

She looked up to see Sally standing before her. Serious and pensive, Sally rolled her head to a cocked position and looked down at Vera's hands.

"Oh ... I know you are so sad, poor thing," Sally said in a low voice, her face long.

There was a pattern here. It seemed at every opportunity, Sally made remarks such as "She is taking it so hard" and "It's hard to know what to do about it. It's heartbreaking to see her this way." All within earshot of Vera.

"Vera? Are you okay?" And Sally pulled out, as if from a top hat, something she juggled in the air and—after some time, with great fanfare—unfolded over Vera's hands. A laminated caterer's menu.

"Here, Vera. Why don't you grab another little corner? Pick out a few more petite sandwiches for the church reception. Did we order enough?"

Vera gawked at her over the laminated menu. "I also didn't know our great-grandmother was a doctor."

"Oh ... you know ... back then being a midwife was like being a doctor. So, who will check the facts on any of it," Sally said hurriedly. "I seriously doubt the newspapers have a fact-checker for obituaries. I don't think they would run a retraction on a dead man's obituary, do you, Vera?" Sally cupped Vera's free hand. "You're sad, and it's hard for you to see the bright side of anything right now, but whether you want to admit it or not, Dad lived a productive and exciting life. People want to know."

Vera was silent.

CHAPTER 9

SEAN

'Tis great confidence in a friend to tell him your faults,
greater to tell him his.

—Benjamin Franklin,
Poor Richard's Almanack

The snap in the air, the still-bracing warmth of the sun silenced them both. It was an Indian summer day in New England: the call for a change in weather and a heightened awareness of time, transition. For some, unsettling in its nature. It was a day before the funeral, and Vera was having lunch, or, as Sean insisted on calling it, a "liquid lunch" (non-alcoholic), even though he was the only one exclusively drinking. They were at an outdoor café in Sean's South End neighborhood of Boston, sitting across from each other at a small round table that took up half the sidewalk. The slightest movement sent the table's wobbly legs into action. The metal chairs were mismatched, collapsible. And the promenading pedestrians too close. An overall uncomfortable setup. But it was all okay because she was with her Sean. Her constant.

She took a breath, savored the draw of cool air as it rushed through her nose to her lungs—feared she may have looked slightly histrionic. Promptly looked down at her sandwich.

"What's that you're drinking?"

"Well, it's supposed to be drinkable. Whipped, blended. Whatever. Yogurt, fruit, and basil ... God, I need a spoon for ... excuse me, be right back ... do you need anything?"

Sean leisurely stood. Elegantly and unhurried, he promenaded to the outdoor self-service stand.

Once, he had advised, "If you do everything slowly, I mean every last thing, no one will ever notice when you do something wrong. It's not the message, stupid. It's the delivery."

She leaned back in her chair, noted its fragility, and watched him. Imagined how if, on the way to retrieve his spoon, Sean were to slip suddenly on a banana peel, he would—after the initial, sudden fall to the sidewalk—lie in repose. Calmly stretch out in place for perhaps a few seconds (an eternity for most); look about, as if slightly surprised, and say, "Damn banana peel." And with his tall, lissome, and sinewy frame, he would carefully and beautifully arise as if demonstrating a new dance move. He'd do it all with an air of aloofness. He'd yawn, as if so blasted bored of the pedestrian onlookers and the sorry sight of them all agog. Sean was never one to scurry.

He slid slowly back onto his seat. If she had slipped on the banana peel, she'd just as well dunk her head into a bucket of ice-cold water with the label fool on it. She needed to listen to Sean more.

A leashed, tiny white fur ball jumped onto Sean's crossed leg. The dog's owner, dressed up for a sashay in her jeans and tweed couture blazer, looked alarmed, frantic really. Sean gathered it up, cuddled with it, and slowly stretched out his long arms for her to take the dog.

"Oh, you are so kind!" she said, and smiled broadly.

"My pleasure. What a cutie," he said, and beamed. They both appeared delighted with each other's friendliness.

Sean was first and foremost a wise person, and Vera loved him. They met in college, late seventies, and had remained close. She worked harder at it than he did. Sean, of course, would have said that was not true. "I love you, Vera. And I always will ... you know, the warts-and-all line ... promise I'll text you first next time."

Sean, Vera, and their friend Jack. The trio had hung out together for four years of undergrad. After college, they all went their own ways: Sean to Berkeley for grad school, Jack to New York to work at Goldman Sachs, Vera to Boston to stumble into a job at an art gallery, working for a billionaire who sold atrocious art at atrocious prices. It was then she took an interest in oil painting. Sean and Jack had never talked about being gay. The freedom of coming out was in its infancy then, even on college campuses, and she had never thought about their sexuality much. Why would she? She was too interested in her own.

After college, the communication mode became letter writing or telephone calls (clocked and charged for every second you spoke). It was easy, commonplace, to lose touch or infrequently connect with dear friends (Facebook social updates wouldn't happen until twenty years later). Two years after they'd graduated, she had received a tearful call from Sean. He couldn't speak at first. All he could croak out, between sobs, was, "Jack is dead. AIDS. He lost his mind and died."

"Listen," Sean said, and Vera blinked, bringing her thoughts away from the past, back to their table in Boston. "I think you've held up incredibly well with all of it. I'll be there for you at the funeral." He gathered a layer of hair and tossed it back from his face with a flair.

He looked down. "Also, I would like to add," Sean said, staring at his hands for too long, "Life isn't fair, so why should death be any different?"

"Ever been with a person dying?"

"No ..."

"Well, let's pick this conversation up after you have."

"Look. I know you said it was intense, grisly. Tell me. Might make you feel better."

"Not ready. I'm a wreck."

"But honestly, you're doing a great job of keeping it to yourself."

"Last thing I want to do. A funeral."

With a gentle look and slow tilt of his head, Sean asked, "Have I taught you nothing, love? You know ... do everything slooooowly ... as if it were meant to be ... you know, what you had intended from the start, and no one will notice if you fuck up or something."

"Thanks for the tip. I'll try to faint in slow motion."

Sean placed one of his hands over her wrist and briefly squeezed it. The table jiggled.

He exaggerated a slow dip with his spoon into the light pink, greenish yogurt. Swirled the spoon around as if searching for something. Took a smidgeon of a mouthful and carefully tucked the spoon alongside the saucer beneath his drink. Pinched the paper napkin from his lap, fluffed it up with a slight snap, and neatly dabbed his mouth. Sean was well-mannered too.

"Don't worry about anything. At this point, it's all over, really. All you have to do is show up for the funeral."

"Well, you know. Always worried about the fainting."

"You are not the damsel-in-distress, fainting type. But I'll be close by," he said.

And she wished Sean would hold her wrist again. They didn't talk for a while. She nibbled on her avocado and sprout sandwich on wheat, and Sean fiddled with his straw, occasionally looking at her with a tender smile.

"I was a terrible daughter."

Sean took a hard look at her. "You were a great daughter."

"Did you read the stupid ... stupid obituary?"

"Like I read the obituaries every day ... well ... okay, I did read it."

"They left out what mattered ... to him ..."

"I must say I was surprised with all his accomplishments. I never knew."

"Total bullshit. I could have, and I should have been involved with writing that up. I just let it go."

"Look. Warren didn't give a rat's ass what anybody thought of him when he was living. Why would he give a rat's ass now?" Sean said. "Stop beating yourself up over nothing."

Taking a deep breath of the fresh air in the bright sunlight, closing her eyes to feel the warmth from the sun on her face, she hoped for some sort of therapeutic relief. Didn't happen.

Sean glanced at his cell phone. "How's this … said writers would like to preface the following obituary with the clear understanding that said departed, does not give a rat's ass what you think of what you are about to read."

"You know, Warren never said anything really like … special to me before he went."

"Like what."

"I don't know. You were special to me …"

"You're joking, right?"

"Well, he told Sally she was a Goddamn fool."

"That's special," Sean said.

"I was with him for a long time …"

"Did you tell him he was special?"

Leave it to Sean to say what she didn't want to hear. She sighed, reminded herself this was one of the reasons she loved him. There was stillness, they never looked away from each other's eyes. She changed the subject.

"Didn't you tell me he could be secretive? Maybe it was one of his big secrets," Sean said.

Warren needed his secrets. Just as Vera needed hers. They both understood this. Sally never did. Warren had always been there for her, after school when possible, weekends. It wasn't until her senior year that he would occasionally stay out all night or go on a fishing jaunt with friends. Vera believed that Warren did the best he could with what he had. From the time she was two years old until just before she left for college, there had been a string of nannies that morphed into part-time babysitters. Vera had attended a private boarding school as a day student. At her school, money and connections mattered. It was donations, gifts, memorials, and trust funds that seemed to warrant the administration's attention. Vera and Sally's inheritance from their mother didn't kick in until they were twenty-one, and Warren could barely pay their tuition. So Vera and Sally were on their own with no leverage whatsoever should they cause a problem. They were also day students, and, from the boarders' perspective, they were just one level above the townies. The boarders ran the show—they were a family. So, Vera's high school education revolved around not getting into trouble and being accepted by the boarders. She knew who to hang with and managed to stay out of trouble by making sure any questionable activities—such as binging on a fine scotch whisky in the school chapel—always included a rich friend or two.

Vera changed the subject.

"Sean. Did I tell you about the great course I took … Athena Redux. It finished up just days before Warren was admitted to the hospital."

"God, no! Not another lecture from your latest seminar. Seriously, Vera. Don't do this to me. I can't stay."

She was irritated. What a jerk Sean could be … so self-centered. She needed this right now. To stay and talk.

With an exaggerated eye roll, Sean tapped the tiny table in

rhythm to make it jiggle. Hummed. "Can we only do the highlights today?" he asked. "About Athena."

"Ok. Athena. She could be a ballbuster, if she didn't like what was happening. Had what the Greeks called *metis*. Basically, social intelligence …"

"Stop. She was a cunning little devil of a goddess … wasn't she?"

"Cunning and scheming can be for good too."

The lunch staff was starting to clean up. She and Sean were the only patrons left.

"Sorry to disappoint, but that's all for today, dear boy."

"Fine. You're not the only lifelong learner, Vera," he said with his silly grin.

Another time, she would share with him that in addition to Athena's high level of metis, the Greeks admired her drive for the unexplained, nameless happiness she was able to cull from particular encounters and relationships.

CHAPTER 10

MR. GAMBLER

Shall we make a new rule of life from tonight:
always to try to be a little kinder than is necessary?

—J. M. Barrie, *The Little White Bird*

Following the liquid lunch with Sean, Vera went home to change her clothes. She had been assigned the pre-funeral afternoon task of picking up copies of the obituary printed on "fine stock" from the printer, with instructions to make sure the lettering was perfect. These were to be passed out at the funeral and church reception. Sally seemed excited to see them.

Before leaving for the printers, Vera stared at her coffee maker for quite some time and thought, "I'm in a terrible state of mind. You know." Without fail, her coffee maker was very special, indeed. She could always count on the coffee maker to listen intently to her—in a nonjudgmental fashion and without giving advice—not to mention satisfying her coffee habit every single morning. The telepathic part was pretty special, too. "I'm stuck in an emotional limbo," she thought, and the coffee maker did its thing, which was nothing. Outwardly, Vera knew she appeared sad, tired and somewhat numbed (as would be expected) and largely seemed to be coping. But she was on edge, exhausted. Her valorous attempts to blunt anything related to what was once called a "nervous breakdown" left her always feeling on the precipice of having one—a complete emotional collapse. At any moment she could go either way. Keep flying or crash. "I'm in a fucking emotional purgatory," Vera thought, facing the coffee maker. "It's maybe worse than just going over the edge and letting whatever happen. You know. Freak out and faint."

Vera sat in the tiny reception area at the printer's office. The room was painted in high-gloss orange with five oversized red plaid chairs lined up against one wall. On the opposite wall, the receptionist talked with a customer through a sliding frosted-glass window. Vera pulled out the original obit from a manila envelope and reread it. Wanted to cry. But she couldn't cry. Couldn't do anything, it seemed. Jesus. She was so feeble and weak, so helpless, so pathetic that Sally and bozo Uncle Nelson had concocted an obituary about Warren that he would have hated. And perhaps laughed at—her only hope of salvation for her cowardly deed (or non-deed): Warren was laughing about this most ridiculous obituary. Ya. He's laughing at this. Must be. Right, Dad?

She suddenly wished she were painting. For the past fifteen years, Vera had practiced the technical aspects of landscape oil painting and found conquering this new skill relaxing, although well aware that her handiwork was totally amateurish. Beginning with memories of landscapes, she progressed to photos and could now set up her easel anywhere outdoors and bask in the compliments of passersby taking peeks. She felt in control of her art. Missed it.

The clerk was busy, talking and motioning with sausage arms and stubby hands. The meaty fingers signaled like tiny, fluttering flags, as if relaying an urgent message. The clerk's face had a stony appearance to it. The expression didn't seem right, didn't seem to fit the face; what should have been plump and rosy with vigor was instead bland and sluggish. Vera saw a tired clerk. Tired.

Dad, this is the craziest thing ever.

She studied the small table next to her. It was low and square, squat. It was meant to look strong and beautiful, with its tabletop of inlaid triangular parquet and four beefy legs standing at attention in what appeared to be oak. But to Vera, it was unsophisticated and artless, a hard-working breed of table. On another day, she might have seen it as beautiful and robust. Today, it was a cheap imitation: gouged and gashed, heaving under stacked magazines and papers, pressed fiberboard held in place with yellowed glue.

She'd left her iPad at home. Spotted a *New York Times* lying on top of the sad table. It was an old one, dated from the previous week, and she picked it up, glanced at the front page. She shuffled to the obituary section as if this were an entirely normal thing for her to do. She scanned each section: paid submissions, death notices, obituaries, and, in the memoriam remarks, there were two elaborate staff write-ups. She gave a sapless sigh. Sally would probably say for years to come how unfair it was that Dad hadn't been written up as a stiff-of-the-day.

One write-up was for a surgeon general, a Dr. William McVain, the other for a newspaper editor, a Mr. Samuel Gambler. There was also a short, paid obituary for Sam Gambler, submitted by members of his church.

First, she skimmed the staff pieces. The dead editor, Mr. Gambler, had it all, it seemed: pedigree, intellect, ambition, the finest education, with achievement and recognition on a national and global scale. There were a few quotes from prior colleagues: "Samuel was intellectually gifted," one said, and "Samuel had many successes in his life," said another.

How did Sam die? Bad luck? Did he have metis? Had he found the joy that would sustain him in his life and through death? Mostly, she wondered about Sam's travelers. Many, just one, or had he gone it alone?

She skipped down to the paid pieces submitted by other friends from work and church: "His sense of humor was legendary, as was his refusal to acknowledge his own importance"; "Sam was a true pleasure to be around and had friends from all walks of life"; "Great heart, unforgettable friend to many"; "He will be missed."

Gently, she folded the paper and placed it on the table. Suddenly felt immense gratitude to the people responsible for submitting these beautiful tributes about Sam Gambler. If she could, she would send off a note—not a text or an email, but a time-consuming, carefully handwritten note, signed, licked, stamped, and mailed—to tell them how much she appreciated what they had shared about Sam. What mattered.

PS And I also want you to know that even though Sam is now dead, I am so happy to know you are still here on earth, and perhaps if you're not too busy you could drop by for a piping hot cup of comforting coffee. I have a very special coffee maker by the way. If you come today, the beans would be a dark roast. Very dark.

Her cell phone vibrated. It was Sally.

CHAPTER 11

MR. MEAD

Out of my own great woe I make my little songs.

—Heinrich Heine,
Out of My Own Great Woe

It was windy with an unusually heavy drenching of constant rain. All day yesterday too. The red, orange, and yellow leaves were beginning to fall from the trees. Brown would soon be everywhere.

Waiting for the funeral to begin, Vera felt like her head was a heavy bucket of sand, and she worried it could topple over. Essentially, another version of her fainting haunts. She had been escorted, basically strong-armed, to her seat by an animated church fixture who sprang into action upon her arrival. He was a huge shuffling sloth of a man, all dressed up, who appeared to do his full best to guide her down the crimson-carpeted aisle: in unison, in keeping with the solemn formality of the event. But his stiff slow strides were out of sync with her hesitant light tap, and they bobbed along for what seemed an especially long time until he plunked her down in the first-row pew of the church. As if this were her choice of seating, to give the audience behind her a clear and unobstructed view: watch the beloved daughter as she grieves or not, holds up or not, keeps it all together or not.

She thought about the crowds who did and still do gather in some parts of the world to watch public executions. Warren wasn't being hung, drawn and quartered, burned at the stake or guillotined—he was being remembered—but still, some parishioners were spectators, merely there to be part of an event, not wanting to be left out, hoping to be seen. No invitation needed. You can't officially crash a funeral. God. She hated her cynicism sometimes.

Beside her, Sally sat erect, staring at the altar. Next to Sally, Nelson reviewed his eulogy notes. Sean was back there somewhere. Where's my best friend?

She was well aware she should look forward toward the altar, like Sally, as if somewhat familiar with and at home within the house of God.

However, she looked up—and was in awe.

The towering ceiling and rich carvings in deepest mahogany took on the feel of a timbered fortress, almighty and safe, bathed in ethereal purple dimness, and she was drawn into the stain glass windows below: pieces of brilliantly colored light—parables in lively relief—each one coaxing her to look to the next and the next. What a joy! To feel a part of this grand creation, so painstakingly and lovingly rendered by the human hand. A mighty draw for religious conversion by all the poor and the wretched living in hovels: a first encounter with the power of fine art infused with a God. And the music! Choirs, with the heavenly song of angels.

Suddenly the funeral began. Took her by surprise. The opening chords of the organ heaved and blasted forth. The choir section stood to sing "Be Thou Thy Vision," and, as if on cue, she found herself rising to a standing position, found herself shoulder to shoulder, soul next to soul, looking directly at the altar.

Be thou my Vision, O Lord of my heart;
Naught be all else to me, save that thou art.
Thou my best thought, by day or by night,
Waking or sleeping, thy presence my light.

Be thou my wisdom, and thou my true word;
I ever with thee, and thou with me, Lord.
Thou my great father, I thy true son.
Thou in me dwelling, and I with thee one.

Riches I heed not, nor man's empty praise,
Thou mine inheritance, now and always.
Thou and thou only, first in my heart;
High King of Heaven, my treasure thou art.
High King of Heaven, my victory won ...

It was a great relief to follow along with the crowd, feel a part of something bigger and more powerful than she. Only needed to do what everybody else did, no one was watching what the lovely daughter would do. They were all singing, looking at their hymnals, the pamphlet, the altar. They were here in sadness and to pay respect. They were beautiful people. Here to mourn and pay tribute to a wonderful man. She felt better.

And there it was. That draw of a familiar power. Trumped her again, just as it had when she was a little girl standing next

to her father and sister, decades ago. She knelt to follow along
with a funeral prayer and watched Uncle Nelson take the pulpit to
deliver Warren's eulogy. Looked down at her hymnal, at the tiny
black print, her hands smoothing over the fragile onion-like paper.
Her hands were clammy and left wet marks on the paper. She
slowly stroked the pages. Found it comforting, somehow. Where
is Sean? She sank down in the pew.

She had been surprised when Warren, on his deathbed, agreed
to have a full funeral, at Sally's insistence. Vera wasn't in the hospital
room when this had been decided, and now, sitting in the church
pew, she tried to beat down the voices of yet another regret. She
had never pursued exactly how Warren wanted to say goodbye. The
strewn ashes. The gravesite gathering. Or nothing at all. Was all this
really what he wanted? She sniffed, the rolling scent of perfumed
and sweaty people in their perfumed and sweaty clothes wafted by,
moist and musty. The word decay popped into her mind, and she
knew it would forever have new meaning for her. Personal meaning.

"Warren *will* be sorely missed *by* me, his only brother, and so
many others ..."
Vera looked up from her hymnal to see Uncle Nelson standing before the podium, a shiny brass eagle with prodigious wings
spread wide. He could have used a few acting classes before
reading the eulogy, because his execution of lasting words was
torturous: it blended the low drone of a faraway fog-horn—stuck—
with a continuous drip drop of words all sounding the same. The
words he emphasized were the wrong ones.

"We were close. *To* lose him so suddenly—is like no *other* pain. What I *will* miss the most is …." Uncle Nelson sniffled, and someone in the pew behind her burped loudly.

Like so many things, the funeral went on for too long. An eternity. She felt best when following the cues—needed the clear instruction: to stand, sit, kneel, and pray. But the signals to act were infrequent because so many speakers had been lined up. She could only sit. Talk to herself. There were the lengthy, undecipherable readings (all selected by Sally), the monotone eulogy by her uncle, the rector's rhetorical semi-sermon, and the separate never-ending organ composition (that clearly had the feel of an intermission). It was hard for her to see how any of it related to her father anymore.

Now, Warren hardly ever attended church, except for Christmas and Easter, a christening, or a funeral. "It's the Anglican Episcopalian way," Warren had once explained to her. "For me, church is more of a tradition than anything." That was after Mr. Mead, the rector, had left us.

Right. Tradition.

But still, she couldn't shake it: the proverbial sting of disappointment in herself, perhaps the beginning of yet another growing contrition. Thank God Sally had gone ahead with the cremation, at least.

A captive, indentured to sit as the funeral dragged on and on, Vera browsed through her thoughts and stopped at a memory from her childhood, the sad story about the kind rector, Mr. Mead. She lowered her head and embellished as best she could. In retrospect, the pair of them had made a comely tableau. Mr. Mead had been scholarly and refined looking with his round Roman collar, narrow and starched white. He was very tall, rounded out with naturally beefy shoulders and always dressed in finely tailored slim-fitting suits—creased and pulled tight across the chest. He had an overabundance of magnificently thick and downy jet-black hair. All he needed was the halo. The congregation adored him. Vera was a tossed about, nothing special kid. A tomboyish, stupid, bright-eyed ten-year-old girl. She had been on the green, hopping about in stacks of dry leaves, her hat and shoes tossed to the side when Mr. Mead had approached, and she remembered the leaves had crackled with her every move.

"What a beautiful orange leaf. In your hair, Vera," Mr. Mead had said.

Her tiny fingers had patted, tugged, and it came out whole, a rubbery, colossal bright orange leaf. She cupped her hands beneath as if it were an offering.

Mr. Mead had picked it up by the stem, held it up to the sun. A frantic church lady came barreling across the lawn. The coffee pot wasn't working.

He had turned to leave. Stopped halfway. "You know, Vera," he'd said. "I think you're a lot like your dad."

She had been dumbstruck. This was a big idea for a ten year old. No one, ever, had said this to her before.

"Make the most of what you can see all around you," Mr. Mead had said. "If you can." He tucked her orange leaf into his jacket pocket.

Then the tragedy. The following Saturday, Mr. Mead's rectory had burned to the ground. "A crying shame," Warren had said a few times. "You'll never meet a finer man than that minister." But he never elaborated or explained, and she had not been allowed to attend the funeral. According to Sally, Mrs. Mead had reported her husband was in his library, preparing for his Sunday sermon, perhaps asleep on his leather couch when the fumes overtook him. This tidbit of information had been of great help for little Vera, as she was able to stop herself from imagining Mr. Mead being burned up alive in the center of a roaring orange and red inferno. She had convinced herself he choked a bit on the smoke and was up in heaven way before the flames hit. Lying on his leather couch, taking a cat nap or something. It was shortly after this tragedy, when they began the religious practice of "tradition": only showing up for Easter, Christmas, and so on.

Uncle Nelson was at the podium again. Reciting a rhyming grade school poem he had written:

"Warren was my brother

I loved him like no other ..."

It was soon after Mr. Mead's demise that Uncle Nelson had shown up one Sunday afternoon and wanted to know why Warren was never at church anymore (well except for the big-event traditions).

"This new rector is a narcissistic pompous prick, and we have better things to do than sit and listen to his nonsensical sermons," Warren had softly replied.

Uncle Nelson had scoffed, "Like you can't be a prick, Warren?"

"Not continuously."

"Did you have an argument or something?" Uncle Nelson had said, his voice loud.

"No. I just figured him out."

Uncle Nelson practically shouted, "It's not all about the minister, you know."

"Isn't it?" Warren had said.

The organ barreled. The congregation thundered out the last stanza from the hymn. She found herself standing and looked up to the altar, balanced and steady, with two enormous vases of oversized deep orange, almost-red tiger lilies. It was over.

The gothic-inspired stone parish hall and the church were connected with a long cloister, which lay beside a squared expanse of leaf-covered lawn. Where's Sean? She definitely wanted to bypass the abbey and avoid the parish hall—the backstage affair after the production where the actors, directors, and audience all mingled about. Another successful funeral service checked off. The talk would be too loud, the camaraderie exaggerated, as the unity broke down into a competition for attention from the rector. Vera couldn't even remember his name. Sally's tea sandwiches would be there.

Sean grabbed her hand, held tightly, and Vera felt the comforting rush of an alliance. The power of his touch, assuring and protecting her. Under his oversized black umbrella, through the drenching rainfall, he tugged her through the tall soggy grass and clumps of leaves, away from the cloister. When they reached his car, she hesitated. She could take off running? Why not? Just keep going. Delight in the cool drizzle down her face—flee into the fog, allow the misty gray shroud to envelop and lead her to nowhere.

"We'll come back for your Beemer tomorrow," he said, pulling open the door of his restored red Karmann Ghia and guiding her down into the front seat.

"How do I open this window," she heard herself say in a gruff tone. She was jittery. Cold.

"Crank window. She's a '74."

Vera left the window closed, and they rode home in silence.

Once at her home, he walked her to her room, said, "Just sleep," pulled off her shoes and cloaked her in the fluffy bed comforter.

That soggy afternoon, Vera dreamt of a burly bear with the head of Mr. Mead. The starched white collar was too small, and it was choking him. He tried to yell across a river of scorching flames and blinding black smoke. She couldn't make out what he was saying for the longest time. Finally, just before she woke up, she heard him.

"Do something, Vera," he wept, big hot tears gushing down his handsome black face.

CHAPTER 12

BLINKY

Never lose your temper, except intentionally.

—Dwight D. Eisenhower

They were enjoying a "liquid lunch" again, this time indoors. The café was busy. Loud. It was two weeks post-Warren's death.

Vera could see him probing within her eyes, trying to measure her mood before he said anything else. "So, you sold your house? Good girl. Closing was yesterday?" Sean's tone suggesting he didn't care whether they continued to talk or sit in silence for the rest of their lunch.

She was happy to be rid of the house. Was tired of the house's lack of selective memory and its unrelenting echo of a previous life she wanted to forget. She had insisted on being present at the closing and was surprised with herself (well, not really, nothing she did surprised her anymore) because she had felt a continuous urge to interrupt and foil the deal. Wanted to shout to the unsuspecting doe-eyed couple, "You don't want to pay this much for my house! You're being gouged, don't you see?" Had to stop herself from jumping up to shake the broker and the attorney—slap the banker. "A young family is being ripped off ... and ... don't you all know ... can't you all see ... I'm going to take the money (along with all the rest) and travel with it, go somewhere far away." With restraint, she had managed to keep from making a crazy ass of herself. Instead, there had been dull small talk and a laboriously slow, regimented passing of papers that were glanced over and signed. It was a long, drawn-out act around the conference table, with the delivery of a raw "caveat emptor" to the sweet innocence and concluded with all participants in a celebratory mood. By the end, she was happy and called her dear friend Astrid to meet for a drink.

"That should give you a few extra pesos," Sean said. "A bonus for holding on to it as long as you did."

"It was the perfect size for Max and me. For just me too ... for all those years."

"Maybe it's a small Cape, but ooh-la-la what a fancy neighborhood!"

"Are you suddenly a real estate agent?"

Sean's expression went blank.

Vera looked at the floor. Stop it. Stop taking this out on Sean.

"Vera. I know this sucks for you. Are you feeling in denial about it all?"

"Denial? If you're referring to the so-called stages of grief, forget it. Leave it to me to jumble them all up anyway. I'm in a rage. Beyond pissed. That's how I feel. No denial anywhere."

"The stages were never meant to be linear ..."

"Right. Well, this is where I am right now," she said.

"Are you angry Warren left you?" Sean asked.

"Oh my God. Have you been boning up on the stages of grief or something?"

"Just wanted to help."

"Who cares what stage of grieving I'm in, really. I'm volatile. In a constant state of flux depending on the circumstances. Mostly angry. And I hate that."

"Maybe denial is next …" Sean said, his words petering out.

Vera scoffed, her eyes rolling upward.

They both looked away from each other. Circled back.

"So, what do you think you'll do now?" Sean asked.

"Been thinking of moving to Greece. Thinking of staying for a few years. Maybe a sleepy little village on Naxos or something."

"Where did Naxos come from?"

"My travel agent—traveled there herself."

"Painting beauteous beaches?"

"If I do this, remind me to ship my linen canvases. Maybe painting will be my way back to coherent thinking."

"Beyond the logistics of getting there—without too much stuff—any plan, any ideas of what you'll do? Not that you need to have any plans, of course." He dipped the tip of his long plastic spoon into the tall glass of yogurt, churned the blueberries on top.

"I don't know. Meet people like you. I want more people like you in my life," Vera answered. "I'm going to make it kind of a mission."

"Oh my God! Another mission? What happened to the art museum … the library … the park plantings … the homeless shelter ... all the church crap with the kids ... auction, after auction, after auction, shipping all those medical supplies to Africa. Oh! And lest we forget my absolute favorite. The student exchange program, where you expected me to be the interpreter for that snotty little French kid for a fucking year! ... Okay ... okay ... so I exaggerated how fluent I was in French."

"This is different, Sean."

"How so?"

"This mission is for me."

"About time."

"... Ever since Dad died, I've been thinking about my own mortality more. A lot more. I know it's a cliché—a tired one—but it's sort of a bucket list."

Sean looked at her, his eyes unnaturally wide open.

"Only instead of things and places to gawk at, my mission is a little more abstract ... I'm on the prowl to find as many meaningful relationships as I can."

"So you can throw away the old ones, I suppose."

"You'll be the first one to go, of course," Vera said with a small but loving smile. "Sean. It's a matter of prioritizing who I spend my time with. I want people in my life who give me something back. The good things. Not the mental turmoil."

"In a race to find as many as you can before you croak?" Sean chuckled.

"Or put the least amount of energy into those where a meaningful relationship is impossible."

"Sounds selfish and narcissistic."

Vera had a short burst of laughter. "Ha! Maybe. But it's all good.

I give plenty of mental stress to the people who give me mental stress. I'm just being proactive. Relieving them of some pain."

Dramatically, Sean stroked his chin, "The ole quality versus quantity perspective, eh? Shared reality and all that."

"With all the people around us, it amazes me how hard it is to find a quality relationship," Vera said.

"Tell me about it! I feel outnumbered all the time. There are so many inept people out there ... they can't fucking do it! Relate. Give you back anything. But it's so cool when you meet someone who can. Isn't it?"

"Ya."

"Secret club or something. Nobody talks about it ... or the members. But they all know who they are."

Sean sipped, she nibbled.

"And you have to go to Greece for this mission? For your painting, I understand. A villa by the sea might do wonders, not that you need it, hon," Sean said. "But the meeting more people like me part, I'm not getting. Do you really think the Greek culture has an abundance of people like *moi*?" he asked, batting his eyes.

"Culture has nothing to do with it, Sean," and she was surprised Sean would not know it was Universal: this social smarts, this metis thing.

"Okay, okay ... I get it," he said. "Identifiable someday by a genetic marker, or something. I know I picked it up in you from the first second I met you, Vera."

"You loved me from the very beginning?" Vera said with exaggerated coyness.

"Hardly. Figured you'd be a pain in the ass forever. But I was drawn to you like you were an addiction. I simply had to have you as my friend."

"I need a fresh setting, and the island sounds lovely."

"Having a drink with Astrid soon," she said.

"Really? Miss seeing Astrid. Love her too, you know. Just not as much as I love you."

"Then off to the MFA. You know Astrid can't sit still for long. Evening hours day."

"What's the exhibit?"

"I don't even know. Doesn't matter."

Sean placed his plastic spoon aside and carefully unwrapped the paper straw. Slid the straw into the concoction: mostly a thin bluish liquid now from all the stormy spoon swirling.

Vera nibbled.

"All I know is this. Some dogs have more of what we're talking about than many people I know ..." said Sean. "Aww ... Mr. Ripley, Mr. Ripley ... I still miss my pooch so much."

Softly, she said, "Poor Ripley ... I miss him too."

"God. You know those two eejits who lived next to me? Barbie and Ken?"

"Ya."

"... and the little silly dog of theirs, the Brussels Griffon ... Coco ... even the name is daffy. The Shit Colored Dog, I like to call it. I know the stupid breed because the only time they stopped to talk to me and Mr. Ripley was when I made a big deal of the Shit Colored Dog because it was a puppy. Of course, all they talked about was Coco this and Coco that. Me this and me that.

Let's just say, Ripley and I were not impressed from the beginning.

"Plus, they got the big picture. That Ripley was sick. That I finally had to put him down—take him out of his misery—and at the same time inflict so much pain on myself.

"How could they not? Ripley and I were inseparable. And all of a sudden, I'm alone on my daily romp. Looking depressed and lost without him. They knew. My other neighbors could see. Said nice things to me—I appreciated it. Their sadness was genuine. I could tell. I always can."

She gently nibbled.

"Ripley, for God's sake, I loved him … Barbie or Ken never said a word to me about Ripley. They're like two robots or something."

Sean took a long sip. Stopped as soon as it turned into a slurping sound.

"I'm beginning to sound morose. Stop me when I do this. Oh, well," Sean sighed. "Mr. Ripley never cared for Konrad or Bernadette or Shit Colored Dog anyway.

"Their loss … they never got to know Ripley. Social eejits."

She nodded in agreement. Reflected on what happened to her earlier in the morning with the eejit at the dog park. And for a second, she considered telling Sean about her recent dog park adventure and what happened—just a few hours before. She could tell Sean, share a story with an appreciative listener. But her embarrassment was still too fresh to share, even with him.

It had happened about nine that morning. Three mornings a week, Vera walked an old black lab—Shadow—as a favor for her neighbor, ending with a romp in the dog park. Vera looked forward to it: the dawdle, the time of day, and she first spotted him from the corner of her eye as she spoke in a low voice on her cell phone, making appointments for a massage and pedicure. She had seen him at the no-leash dog park countless times: courteously smiled at him, extended pleasantries about the weather, ignored the skittishness of his underfed dog (what was the dog's name ... Blinky?), and instead mentioned the unusual coloring (quite ugly, truthfully) of Blinky's coat. All to no avail. Hey, she tried. Her cell had a poor connection, and she was having a hard time catching everything said to her when the eejit, the little ass, began shouting and gesticulating.

"HEY. YOU THERE. Your dog is defecating!" he yelled at her. She was clearly still talking on her cell phone.

"YOU! DO YOU HEAR ME? GET OFF THE PHONE! NOW!" he shouted, both arms in the air, thrashing Blinky's leash around as if Vera hadn't seen or heard him by now. The leash whipped out of his hand and landed on the gravel, dusting up a gritty powder.

"Hello, yes, I'll need to call back later," and she pocketed her cell.

"What's all the fuss?" she said, winding up Shadow's leash.

"YOUR dog is defecating. YOU need to pick it up!"

She looked at Shadow. Poor thing was straining to poop. The dog looked embarrassed.

"As if I'm not going to pick it up." Vera rolled her eyes.

He had a bellicose air. About forty or so and already beginning to bald, he had a slight pudginess about him—most likely misconstrued as the body of a hearty athlete each time he strutted by the mirrors at the local upscale health club. His rounded tortoise glasses, waxed canvas jacket, and leather leash were a triangle of brown hues, rain or shine. The one time she had heard him speak during a very brief conversation with her, answering a simple question about his dog, she had clearly detected affectation.

As Vera bent down to scoop up Shadow's poop, she said calmly, "I know you…. I've seen you; you've seen me—here, with our dogs—countless times. Of course, I'll pick up after my dog."

Shadow was done. The little man looked at the poop (it was steaming).

"I was making an appoint …"

"Pick up the shit." He strutted off.

Vera had always prided herself on not swearing. All through prep school and during college (even summer camp), when surrounded by peers spouting their crude obscenities—*shit, asshole,* and, of course, the perennial favorite—*fuck*—Vera would say things like *what the heck, oh gosh,* or *darn.* She rationalized her uncool, prim discourse by arguing (in her own mind) that having such a grand command of intonation, timed interjection, and facial expression, with even with the dullest of words, she could zing as well as any fool with a chest full of swears. It became a game for her—make the point, shock 'em, wake 'em all up—without the need to ever say the word *fuck.* She was proud of this somehow. Also, knew it qualified her for therapy.

The dog poop steamed.

"Fuck you," she yelled.

The little man stopped and turned. He looked stunned.

"Did you hear me, you eejit! I said, 'Fuck you. You eejit,'" Vera bellowed.

"And … your wimp ass dog."

"Fuck you."

"No, FUCK YOU!" Vera roared.

The little man's head bobbed about fiercely, his eyes blinked. He croaked out a weak syllable, "Moth—"

She cut him off.

"YOU ARE A FUCKING DUMBASS!" She was out of breath, her face throbbed red.

"... er Fu—"

"DUMBASS. Fucker."

As if on cue, they both halted and stomped away, an enraged pounding strut in opposite directions, as if to say, the duel now begins. She called to Shadow, and the dog scrambled to the car. She noticed—with delight—that the little man had bumbled off in the wrong direction and had to retrace his steps to retrieve Blinky's leash and pass by her again to reach his car. Dumbass.

As she opened her car door, she delivered the final blow.

"Who but a total loser ... would name a dog BLINKY!"

He kept his head down, skulked by with the little dog.

As she sat in her car, the thought actually crossed her mind to smear the dog poop (held in a plastic bag—still warm) all over his fucking car. She could pick out his car. But the little man, this little fucking dumbass, would press charges or something, and the other dog walkers would testify: "Yes. I saw her blue BMW at the dog park in the morning." And she would end up having to recount every detail of her encounter with the little man, and no, she could never take the stand and admit to such profanity, admit to such shouting and yelling in a dog park, all because the little man was a fucking little dumbass. She started up the car. Plus, she could never say the f-word on the stand.

Vera nodded her head at Sean, in agreement with whatever he had just said. I'll tell Sean about Blinky another time, she said to herself.

"It's amazing … seems like they are everywhere sometimes … the Kens and the Barbies," Sean said.

"Not sure when I'll leave yet, Sean. Soon, though. And please, no going-away gala. Who knows, I could be back in a week. We'll see what happens."

Sean swallowed hard, flung his hair back, and pointed his chin up. "If you don't have some sort of bon voyage gathering, people will wonder."

"Wonder what?"

"Oh. I don't know. Maybe wonder if you've skipped away to heal from a mental breakdown … cosmetic surgery or something. People have wild imaginations, you know."

"Fuck them."

Sean froze.

"What?" he said. "You're blowing my mind here. I've *never ever* heard you utter this particular word, my sweet little complicated girl."

"There's a new swearer every day, you know," she said with a sly smile.

"I suppose it's your day, your moment, your coming-out party, of sorts … to join our club of swearers, who make up ninety-nine point nine percent of the human population—even the bonobo monkeys have their own way of saying *fuck*, for fuck's sake. Oh my. To think, here today, such a monumental occasion happened with little ole me. I feel so privileged. Well, fuck me!"

They both laughed, and their eyes spoke to each other. She could see Sean see she was sad to leave him (sadder than he).

"You always make wise decisions, my gray-eyed dove."

"Dove. Really? I'd rather be a gray-eyed warrior."

She decided when telling Sean about the dog-park episode and how she had shouted *fuck* multiple times, she'd change the timeline. She wanted Sean to think he had been the first.

CHAPTER 13

REVELATIONS ON THE GREENWAY

Great quarrels often arise from small occasions but never from small causes.

—Winston Churchill,
My Early Life: A Roving Commission

Vera called them Sally walks. Infrequent and intense.

A month after the funeral, it was sunny and mild—one of those spectacular fall days in the Northeast that no one can really understand unless they've had the privilege of living it. Sally wanted to meet up at the north end of Boston's Greenway and walk part or all of the two-and-a-half-mile connecting park system, after picking up her special candied Turkish pistachios from Boston's Quincy Market.

Vera made her way under the massive steel pergola to the Armenian Genocide memorial and spotted Sally sitting beside the water fountain sculpture. Enormous, polished black granite and multisided, the sculpture was a tribute to the everchanging immigrant experience and was reconfigured each year. Vera made a point of seeing each year's particular shape. She'd go alone, sit close enough to hear and feel the spraying mist from the water-fall, and reflect on a year gone by, time, and impermanence. Then meet someone for a stiff drink.

"Hey!" Sally said, sucking on a pistachio. "Somehow I ended up at the carousel first. Those animals, insects, whatever the kids ride on are so creepy. What little kid would want to ride on a gross grasshopper?"

Vera thought they were beautiful, imaginative works of art. "Carousel will be shutting down for the winter soon," she said.

Never really at ease on "the walks," Vera was also uncomfortable due to her predilection for always looking up. A head taller than her sister, in order to appear attentive, she had to look downward to Sally.

This difference in height was yet another fact Sally would occasionally point out to Vera. "I'm the exact same height as Mum, you know ... from the picture," she'd say. "I figured out her height from deducting her heels and comparing her to Dad's actual height. Looks about two inches. Dad isn't that tall. Where did you get your height from?" Sally would say. "Kinda strange." And Vera would whisper to herself: you're a fucking mathematical genius, Sally (before the Blinky dog park debacle, Vera often said the F word, but only to herself).

They set about, and Sally sped up upon approaching the car-ousel. The yellow striped tent at the top went slowly around, and if Vera were alone, she would have sat on a bench and watched for a while.

"So many memories about Dad pop up every now and then," Sally said.

"Ya."

"He was kind of secretive about where he was, what he was doing, a lot. You know. When we got older."

"You mean his fishing trips and all."

"Like all the nights he never came home. And then when he finally did, it was pretty obvious he had a major hangover."

Vera laughed. "Remember the time he came down from upstairs—for breakfast—with that hungover woman in the bee-hive-like hairdo following him?"

"That's what I mean. Where had he been? Who was she? What did they do together the night before?" Sally said.

"Oh my God. That table, with the four of us sitting around trying to have a conversation."

"And then you said you liked her hair!" Vera laughed.

"Remember what Dad said after she left?" Vera grinned. "I've seen some bad hairdos in my days, but geez."

"Yes. He had secrets," Vera said. "Or valued his privacy. Maybe he told us what we needed to know. That's all. Deepened the love we had for each other by giving us space. We did the same for him … gave him space."

"Ya. I didn't really give him space," Sally said. "I just got tired of asking him questions he really never answered…."

"If Dad had told us every little bitty thing about where he was, with whom, what he did, what was he thinking, all that noise would have gotten in the way somehow. He didn't need to share everything. I just trusted his ability to filter what was best for us to know and best for us not to know."

"He could have filtered telling me I was a Goddamn fool," Sally said.

They headed to the Wharf District, past the Rings Fountain and fading flowers, and at the Fort Point Channel area with its large-scale art installations, Sally cleared her throat and made an announcement.

"I've found Jesus," Sally said.

"Really? Where's he been hiding?" Vera said.

"You know, Vera, I knew I could never talk with you about this."

Vera was surprised by her response to Sally. The fast-paced marches usually played out with Sally talking most of the time, and Vera not saying much. Vera could be a good listener. During the Sally walks, Vera had learned it best to suppress whatever she happened to be thinking in order to avoid confrontation: getting into it, arguments, fights, feeling worse at the end of the ramble than at the beginning.

Fuck's sake. That wasn't very nice of me to say to Sally. Where's Jesus been hiding. Nice. At least didn't call her a God-damn fool. Out loud, anyway …

Sally's sunk-in chest twitched, and she barely breathed out. "Sure," she said. "I had to listen to your big idea about being a Buddhist. And where did that all go? So self-centered."

"Ah … how did you, a … become a Jesus follower?"

"Amazing, really. I was talking with Mrs. Hooper, our old neighbor, on her front lawn. Stopped by to thank her for writing such a nice note on the website for Dad's obituary. So, there we were, and like from out of nowhere, two really nice women showed up. Really nice. They were there to offer condolences to Mrs. Hooper and see if she needed any help or anything. Mr. Hooper died last month, remember. So, Mrs. Hooper introduced me and mentioned about Dad and the women knew all about it because they read the obituaries every day. Anyway, they remembered his! Thought it was well written. Can you believe that? One just got back from an aid mission in Africa. They were so sad about Mr. Hooper and Dad too. I could tell it was genuine."

"Did they have briefcases?"

"I give up. This is what you want to know. Did they have briefcases? Really, Vera?"

"Remember what Dad said. Anyone that shows up on your doorstep with a briefcase is usually not there in your best interests."

Sally picked up the pace considerably with the longest rhythmic strides it appeared that she could manage.

"Well, what do you believe? Tell me," Vera said.

"Jesus was crucified for us and rose from the dead."

And Vera felt the pressure to respond. She thought of herself as a Christian. Sort of heeded the Ten Commandments (the important ones) and learned all the parables. Sure, there was a guy named Jesus, and he was pretty spectacular, but the "Jesus rose from the dead" part was a bit too much. Once, while a teenager at a summer camp in Maine, she somehow ended up in a small group discussion about faith. The group's leader was also a teenage girl who had an egg-shaped torso, with legs too long and too skinny. She displayed a wide yellow sash diagonally across her rounded chest with multiple cloth badges, all sewn on by hand and slightly crooked. Most of the badges had tiny crosses hiding somewhere in them. She had a serious nature and informed the participants that in order to consider yourself a Christian, you had to believe in the resurrection literally.

"Totally," she had said, and rubbed her badges. Vera asked if a metaphorical interpretation of the resurrection met the standard. "What's a metaphor?" the girl had said. No. Sally would not appreciate hearing this little story, and Vera continued to walk in silence.

"I wonder if we were like … too impatient with Dad," Sally said. "When he was in and out of it. The babbling. You know. The gasping-for-air part. When he couldn't catch his breath for so long, and he was kinda fitful. That's all part of it, Vera. God makes us, and only God can take us away. God specifically asks us not to be impatient in the end," Sally said.

Vera's felt her nostrils flare. She came to an abrupt stop, held Sally back with her arm, and Vera looked down to her, head on.

"Don't start that 'prolonging life at all costs' shit with me. I don't know what sect of Christianity you belong to. You can believe in whatever you want. No one. Absolutely no one on this earth can say for certain whether a person in that state feels pain. Do they feel as if they're slowly suffocating? Drowning? Having one panic attack after another? Very possible. We did the compassionate thing, erred on the side of caution. What we should be thanking God for … is Dr. Cooke. And the scientists that developed morphine."

"Well. I appreciate your honesty."

So mature for Sally to say such a thing. And that word—honesty—appeared to Vera in the shape of a holy stepping-stone meant for her to take and rise up. And she did. Simple honesty. Energized, armed with the aegis of truth, and feeling brave, Vera grabbed the seat on a nearby rusted green bench.

Side by side, eyes level, Vera searched Sally's eyes, looked for confirmation that she could continue. With the truth.

"Sally. You and I are so different. It's been hard for me sometimes to say what I really feel about things you say or do—don't want to hurt your feelings or argue all the time like Dad and Uncle Nelson."

"Like I don't know we're different," Sally scoffed. "You and Dad were like two peas in a pod. Me? Always on the outside. Never got your sense of humor. Never got a lot of things … you and Dad did."

"Never meant to exclude you."

"I couldn't say half of what I thought when we were together," Sally said. "Got better when I was older. Trained myself to ignore whatever you said or did. Like never pressuring Dad about where he was or what he did. Your expectations of people are so high, Vera, and I know I never met yours. Or Dad's. Hardest part was never getting the jokes you both found so hilarious."

They sat on the bench and looked down for a while. Vera brushed off the peeling green paint stuck to her hand.

"Wonder if I'm like Mom," Sally said, speaking in a calm, sweet voice as if all was forgiven.

"Oh, you must be. What with the height, blue eyes and all," Vera chirped. "Don't you carry that photo of Mom and Dad in the special frame with you at all times?"

Sally smiled. "Where did you come from? You don't look like Dad or Mom."

"Fuck off," Vera said.

"No, you fuck off."

They laughed, Sally's laugh louder, more boisterous than Vera's. Sally draped her arm over Vera's shoulders and gave a little shake. Maybe this finding Jesus would be a good thing.

CHAPTER 14

CAMILLE'S RED KIMONO

It's about time that we accepted total celibates as no more deranged, inefficient, unhappy or unhealthy than any other section of the population.

—Germaine Greer

The following week, Astrid called. Suggested the Boston Museum of Fine Arts. Evening hours. Cocktails first. "You need to chill," she had told Vera.

It was early on a Friday night; Astrid and Vera sat at the far end of the bar. A sudden heavy rainfall had started outside. The Oak Room at the Copley Plaza was well known for its classic polished feel: lacquered mahogany bar, scaled for a room five times larger; with just enough lighting from tiny shaded lamps to make every patron look mysterious and unforgettable; and a glorious display of liquor bottles bathed in ice-blue light that went all the way to the ceiling. The sound of pounding rain seemed to go with the script.

Astrid took a sip of her scotch.

"How we doing, Vera?"

"Doing," Vera said. "I'm slowly emerging from the dark side. It helps to know you're there, Astrid."

"Another drink?"

"Should be doubles," Vera said.

Astrid motioned to the bartender. He sashayed over, cool and juvenile, out of place with the stuffiness of the surroundings.

"Again, please … your Pimm's Cup okay, Vera?" Astrid asked.

"Doubles on the Lagavulin and Pimm's No. 1," Vera answered.

"Why the doubles? Something we should be celebrating?" Astrid said, scanning the room for anyone she might know.

"Two years today, my divorce."

"Happy to see you celebrating. At last," Astrid said, her eyes circling back to Vera's.

"Hard to believe Max died just last year. So sudden. What was it again?"

"Aneurysm. Bled out in his brain. Was swimming in the Bimbo's pool. Bled out and drowned."

"You always told me he died in her arms."

"Well, after they fished him out of the water."

"Still blame the big D on sex, or have you finally come to the realization Max was just an ass?"

"'Twas the sex."

"Vera. You're free."

Vera fingered the strawberry and cucumber garnish on her drink. Max, an ass? She summed up their divorce in one word: sex. He wanted more of it, she didn't. She took full responsibility for her actions: she wasn't going to do what she didn't want to do. Again, and again.

Max had been fine with it for a while. They had so much else together: fun and laughter, respect and concern for one another. There was always a sweet tenderness flowing between them, mutually recognized with a touch here and a look there. They stumped every marriage counselor as to any "problem" until they hit the sex subject. At that point, it always seemed to take a turn for the worse (for her).

The counseling sessions had always started out on a big happy note, finding the commonality between Max and her: morals, interests, sports, hobbies—evolving into politics and philosophies of life. Second stage came the exploration of an endless list of activities for them to do together if they weren't already doing so: volunteering for the same cause, hiking, golf, cycling, travel, theater, chorus, fly fishing, scrabble, photography, paddle boarding, and her favorite—binge-watching series on their flat-screen television. This stage morphed into the all-important activity of sex, pretty fast. And it was always then that the looming dark abyss of divorce emerged. In hindsight, she truly believed during the sexual activity discussion phase, she should have heard a supportive comment along the lines of "you are okay" or "you are not the one who needs to change, Vera" or "what you feel is common for a woman at your stage of life." Instead, she heard the opposite, with the clear insinuation that something was not quite right with her, without anyone ever saying the word abnormal.

"Ya, well ..." Vera said to Astrid, and picked at the cucumber slice in her drink. "If you remember, I tried to talk with you about him.... Many times."

"When?"

"Our long walks. All my girlfriend coffees and cocktails?"

"All you talked about was sex! Not Max."

"Well, who do you think I was alluding to?"

"Well ..." Astrid said. "I probably got a little confused when you started in about scientific studies and hormones ... I thought ... what the? ... don't want to discuss and debate about everything...."

"Yeah, and thanks for helping me with my sex rally idea," Vera said.

"Vera. Honey. We've been over this. We thought you were losing it. Do you remember me trying to talk you out of it?" Astrid said. "We decided not to enable you. For your own good. What time does the museum close?"

What had happened was this. Vera became empowered after the divorce: a soldier for her own sexual needs (or lack thereof)—in a delusional sort of way. Through the process of defending herself in every counseling session, she came to sanction her own truth, and she had liked the feeling. Hey, an educated, independent person living in a time of great excitement for women, she could say and do what she liked. She didn't live in a country where a woman's only worth was to please men, make babies, have a miserable life, and die. She could voice her new societal perspectives anytime, anyplace, and with anyone (well, in free countries anyway) who would listen to her.

But nobody was getting it. Everyone wanted to talk about something else, and in retrospect, she had to agree with Astrid: she'd lost it.

A year ago, just before Max suddenly died, Vera had woken up with a peculiar bravado one fine sunny morning and asked Astrid and Skye to help her set up a "Just Say No to Sex" rally. She suggested they rent a bullhorn, podium, even a tent. Post it on the internet, time and place. But Astrid and Skye were not interested and tried to redirect her to an idea that wasn't crazy and then Vera started having dreams about how the things might go. One was a recurring nightmare of her at the rally, tap dancing on stage, with her shoes the weight of dumbbells, singing and saying something stupid that everybody laughed about for weeks. In another dream she was, on a rainy day, yelling to mostly homeless people who had lunched at the nearby shelter. One of them shouted for her to sing, and she had briefly frozen. But a few of them did cheer her on. So Vera gave up on her plan for a rally.

"Yeah. Well again, thanks for all the support." Vera took a sip of her drink.

"We were trying to protect you. Ha-ha …" Astrid said, smiling. "We used to love those impersonations you did of people … you know … from the Viagra commercials. So funny."

The boy-faced bartender, pretending to be hip, arrived with drinks. "I doubled for the double order," he said to Astrid and slid his arms over the bar with his hands folded until his face was inches from Astrid's. "What you asked for … right … no charge, of course."

Astrid smiled at him. "We'll take the check, please." She turned to Vera and said in a loud, frightened voice, "Rocky's angry and has mental issues. Whenever he sees me with anyone—he gets kinda crazy, you know?"

Vera rolled her eyes. The bartender's arms slithered back, and he disappeared.

Vera smirked and chuckled, wished he had tried to flirt with her.

"But honestly, Carlton was an ass of a husband too," Astrid said. "You know what seriously pissed me off? All the write-ups making him out to be some kind of a fucking hero because he came home from work, stretched into his pretentious name-brand bike clothes—with the special little logos all over—and took off for hours and hours. Devoted like four or five hours a day to himself. Narcissism in disguise."

"I never got it all out back then—you know—with the speak-of-the-dead rule and all," Astrid said. Sipped. "He was the worst kind of recreational athlete jerk. Nothing was more important to him than his body and how he performed … as if he were a contender for the Olympics or something."

Vera had first met Astrid at a volunteer organization, almost twenty years before. Astrid was already a widow. Her husband had died from attempting to cycle over a sizable pothole—with a subsequent nasty fall. She had promptly adopted two toddler boys from foster care, now both young adults: one black, one white. Thanks to Astrid's nagging, there had been a substantial life insurance policy in place; word got out about the bounty, and suitors lined up. She never remarried. "It would have to be a young, brilliant stud for me to be attracted—and satisfied—and that ain't gonna happen," Astrid liked to say.

The rain hadn't let up. Astrid texted for a ride.

"I don't have an umbrella or anything."

"So, we'll run," Astrid said, squeezing into her short red leather jacket and zipping up the gold oversized front zipper where it stuck just below her bountiful breasts.

They stood outside, beneath the burgundy hotel canopy. Vera licked the fruity flavor and gin from her lips, inhaled the rain's earthy scent. She was buzzed: she singled out the distinctive pelting sound of the heavy rainfall and the unrelenting fury of the tiny droplets—as if they had been trapped in the clouds for too long and finally set free. The car arrived, and without a word, Astrid sprinted to the black suburban, hands covering her hair and face, not an easy task with her heels.

Vera stood beneath the sogged canopy. Each droplet plunged to the gritty sidewalk and splattered into a spray, leaving dotted imprints on her flat, peach-colored suede shoes. Her ankles were wet with cold, and her whole body shivered. Wished she had worn pants. The open door of the black SUV waited. She leapt to run straightaway, like Astrid had, but Vera looked up, and as the heavy beads walloped her face, it all felt right—as if the elements were finally together again—and she was so happy for them: the black clouds, the air a chilling cold, the soaking rain. She ambled to the open door, climbed in with a little help from the driver. Yup. She was slightly drunk.

"Out for a stroll?" Astrid said, and laughed. Pushed her elbow against Vera's.

The driver stopped at the museum entrance on Huntington Avenue, and Astrid snatched Vera's hand, galloped through the dim wet to the vast double oak door. Vera smoothed her hand over the jagged cracks of the damp, roughhewn wood, and she had a fuzzy intoxicated shock over the enormity of the black steel hinges.

Something ominous about the doors. Sinister. Something missing.

"Needs a placard in calligraphy," Vera said. "Abandon all hope, ye who enter here." Was pleased she didn't slur her words.

Astrid laughed, yanked open one of the hulking doors, pulled Vera inside, wiped the wet from her leather jacket, and wrung out Vera's dripping ponytail. They took a breath and looked upward to the long staircase. Vera hesitated, as if at the base of a snow-covered peak, preparing herself mentally for the challenging hike ahead. Her thoughts scattered.

"We can't go in like this," Vera said. "I'm drunk."

"Slightly. Anybody asks, we just came from the pool. Thirty-five laps. Best time ever."

They grabbed the center brass railing between them—Vera to steady herself. Astrid paused and took the first step, set the pace. Vera kept up with the rhythm, and they painstakingly climbed the stairs, Vera in her drenched flats, Astrid in her heels. Halfway up, Astrid turned to look down and briefly halted. Vera kept the pace this time, and it was Astrid who caught up.

They reached the landing of the soaring rotunda and stood directly across from Singer Sargent's fresco of the wise goddess Athena. The goddess was faintly colored, her armor protecting architecture, painting, and sculpture from the ravages of time. Her eyes, an honest penetrating gray. And so there she was, Vera Mine, divorced, single, and free. Fatherless. Standing in the very center of splendor, yet on the edge of a free fall for what was to come: the beauty of artistry, the quest for meaning. A dulled exhilaration overcame her. Ya, the alcohol helped.

"We don't have a lot of time," Astrid said. "Should we split up?"

"—in the mood for Monet."

"I'll check out the new exhibit, circle back to you."

Boston had an impressive permanent gallery dedicated to Monet. Vera had often spent hours at a time in the Monet room. She headed to her cushy round ottoman in the center of the room—*La Japonaise* was still showing. It was a large-scale painting of Monet's wife Camille in a jarring red silk Japanese kimono, fanning her face, looking directly at the viewer and her husband. She wore a blond wig and had a cheerful face. Each time Vera studied it, she found herself rushing through Monet's technique and skill to wonder about Claude and Camille as people and their relationship with each other. Camille had been his beautiful teenage model and lover. She died at thirty-two from a botched abortion or cancer—was never clear. There were always questions about how he treated her. Did they have metis? Had they been travelers for each other?

Scanning the gallery, she saw only one patron. Friday nights were fabulous. She settled farther into the plush purple ottoman with gold braided fringe touching the floor and smoothed her hand over the velveteen. So soft. So right to be here.

One day while at home, over the course of Warren dying, Vera oddly found herself leafing through one of her art books to find Monet's portrait of *Camille on Her Deathbed*. It was the same painting that had come to mind earlier, when she sat in the hospital room looking at Warren. She had visited Paris's Musée d'Orsay decades before, and at the time she had been horrified by it, couldn't venture beyond Claude's hopeless swirls of grays, blues, and yellows—with a brush of red. But now, as she sat on the ottoman and stared across to Camille's lively, blushing face, she thought about his two paintings and had a new appreciation for how Monet had indeed captured the moments of Camille in both life and death.

She studied the lavish kimono Camille wore. Did the old goat Claude have her dress up in other outfits for him? God knows. Poor thing. No marriage counseling in her time. The embroidery was extraordinary.

Heavenly God. Stop. Stop. Associating everything with dickhead Max. The counseling was good, though: had helped her verify what she had suspected all along and helped her understand what she wanted.

Vera wished she could curl up on the ottoman. Nap.

The final attempt at counseling—the descent of no return—had been with an earnest flabby-faced counselor named Joan. Joan had an unusually large head, topped off with a long oily mop of brown-and-yellowed white hair, perpetually yanked back with a colorful, too-large scarf.

Joan's physical minutiae were distinctly remembered because, by the end, Vera had surreptitiously stopped listening to the counseling and instead kept a close eye on Joan's dangling earrings and such. The hefty earth-colored beads tumbling down to clip her broad shoulders, twitched every time she appeared revved up. As expected, the sex problem was broached.

Joan had a percussive pattern to her delivery. Short sentences, variable only by the force of her strike on the drum or cymbal.

"Think. About changing. Vera," Joan had said, and wiggled

her turkey neck. "You could. Please your partner. It's something. You can. Should do." She cocked her head back, exposing nostrils too large and rounded for her beak-like nose.

"It's fair. This is not. An unreasonable request. From your husband. There are. Many remedies available. To increase your sexual drive. Vera. Hormones, toys, self-help books, videos. There are. Whole stores. Catalogs. Devoted to … this." (She remembered Max had nodded his head enthusiastically with this.)

"Every marriage. Requires two flexible partners. It all comes down to unselfish sacrifice," she had said, and Vera remembered how Joan's nostrils were full of black hairs, all crisscrossed.

Wow. Unselfish sacrifice. At the time, she had considered throwing in the towel right then and there: march out on them, call Astrid or Sean to meet for a drink. She had never really associated sex with sacrifice—she being the sacrificial lamb, and well, her dignity and all—and okay, she could be selfish. Selfish when it came down to knowing the difference between what great sex had been for them and the sad imitation variety. Sure. She could have pretended. Could have.

The beat of Joan's voice had taken on a melody. Simple and still boring, but it woke Vera up.

"Vera?" Joan had said. "Have you ever heard of the new drug out called flibanserin? It increases a women's desire to have sex."

"You seem angry, Vera." Joan had said.

"Any side effects?" Vera asked. "Stroke. Heart attacks. Frequent and sudden desires for sex with my refrigerator?"

"Okay, Vera. We get it. You don't like the idea of taking a new drug," Max had barked.

"We can work with this," Joan had said, and bobbed her earring in circles for a while. Looked at Max.

Vera felt a friendly elbow as Astrid casually sank into the ottoman.

"That needle dick of a bartender, gave us more than doubles. Doubling the doubles meant he gave us four shots a drink. I thought he was joking. Tasted strong, but Jesus. I need to sleep." Astrid plopped her head onto Vera's shoulder. Arm in arm, they stood, holding each other up.

Vera said, "Ya, so. It was a combination. Max and sex."

"What …"

"Your question … was the divorce because of sex … or was Max just a jerk."

"I had a dwindling libido, and Max wanted what I couldn't … didn't *want* to give him anymore," Vera said.

"Maybe your libido will perk up with another man."

"Doubt it."

"Look, you refused to be a damn performing sex slave. I respect you for that, Vera. Hey, best part is the final absolution. Two years ago, today. I'll text for the car."

With all her confidence and strength to "go it on her own," it helped that Vera had the means to support her present lifestyle. Without this, who knows what she might have put up with.

"What day you leaving for Greece?"

"November first."

Vera's thoughts revolved around how much she loved Astrid.

It had been the happiest day for Vera since Warren had died.

CHAPTER 15

RIDING HIGH

Oh, I get by with a little help from my friends.

—John Lennon and Paul McCartney

"Here. You need this," Astrid said.

The museum excursion was just last week. It had taken Vera an entire day to recover from her hangover.

Riding along in the back seat of Skye's slick black SUV, Vera took a deep breath through her nose, and her highly sensitive nostrils twitched from the permeating spice of marijuana, mixed with the leathered scent of a new car. She pinched the burning joint between the tips of her slender fingers, held it up, twisted it, looked at it sensibly: as if she had never seen one in real life before, or as if after careful review she might just say no to drugs and pass it back to Astrid. It was soon, maybe too soon since Warren's death (six weeks to the day), and yet after having had a few drags, Vera discovered it had been too long—over thirty years now—since she had last smoked weed. Hello old friend. She brightened up.

It was Astrid's idea to go away to her family's lakeside "hut" for the weekend. "It will do us all good," Astrid had told her. "We'll get away, be together. Plus, I can take a break from my bullshit legal work."

"What if I have a paranoid episode?"

"You won't," Astrid had informed her. "And the lake is beautiful in the fall. The color will last for only a few more days. The silence there can be cathartic."

At first, she wasn't sure about going. Be there, that's all. She found this thought helpful with the events she simply had to attend, and in this case, all she had to do was show up, smoke a few joints, eat a few brownies, say as little as possible. Wouldn't need to say anything interesting or particularly witty, wouldn't need to say anything at all. Nothing was expected of her.

Though she couldn't blink away one thought. Recreational pot laws were constantly changing from state to state. Who knew what New Hampshire's were? She had dreamt about it: being led away in handcuffs and prosecuted by some crazy federal lawyer who wanted to make an example of them—their lives, their careers, the four women of Newton, in ruins.

Vera's career? Right. Master's degree in psychology. Good luck to anyone with that degree. She was fired from her position as an adjunct professor for intro psychology courses after five years. Or not asked to return. There was a big kerfuffle about her students not doing so well on the final exam. Of course, it didn't help that her peer had been named professor of the year, twice. After looking at the stats over a five-year period, they were certain that Vera was the problem. She had tried to explain her teaching method: allowing the students to direct where the discussions went. But she gave up after the dean sternly said her role wasn't to be a moderator or discussion facilitator, she had been hired to teach the students something they didn't already know. Vera remembered she had left his office, sad—about being fired and not having a job, of course. But sad, mostly, about feeling that perhaps the problem was indeed her—she had nothing to teach the students. Didn't know pretty much anything about anything.

Skye asked if anyone wanted a car window down. "Too smoky for anyone?"

"Aww ... Skye ... the eternal social worker," Astrid said playfully. "Always worried about everybody else."

In the front seat, Jane said, "I can barely breathe," and slid her window all the way down. A fierce blast of air sucker punched Vera and Astrid in the face. The joint torpedoed to the floor of the car.

"Hey. Not so far down!" Astrid shouted. "Jeez, Jane."

Jane put her window up, leaving half of it open. "It's so smoky," she said. "It's making me cough. A lot."

Jane was newly married to Skye's brother, and a number of times, Vera (at Skye's invitation) had joined her and Jane for coffee, lunch, and movies. Vera found Jane to have an especially serious nature. Was quiet and unassuming.

Vera re-tied her hair back, kept the front strands from lashing her in the face.

Astrid picked up the joint, relit it, and the remaining journey to the hut was magical to a stupefied, stoned Vera. As they traveled farther north, the fall leaves that hadn't dropped from the trees yet became alive—a moving kaleidoscope of color—ever changing, almost dizzying at times (or maybe it was Skye's driving, she had always been a crazy driver). Along the way, only a few thoughts of doom were stifled: once when the red and orange leaves hanging from the trees suddenly became a study in plant life, and the brilliance—the joy of their color—only a sad consequence of leaves dying. Later, she smothered her thoughts when the brown crinkled leaves on the ground suddenly stirred up bright orange flames from decades ago—whirling around Mr. Mead as he stood on the church lawn, lining up to burn in a perfect circle around him. The ring of fire spread fast, in shape and dimension, as more dried leaves joined in—all grinning in wait for their cues to ignite. Yup. Here she was—over forty years after the tragedy—praying Mr. Mead had died without the withering pain of burns: asleep on the couch in his small study, surrounded by his books. He simply coughed on smoke and died. She closed her eyes. Felt the cool gust of wind from Jane's partially opened window and imagined herself on a sailboat, cruising along for pleasure with a competent captain. This will be okay with my Astrid and Skye—everything will be okay. All good.

As usual, Astrid had been right. The hut getaway was already helping. Since the funeral, Vera's rage had slowly turned into denial. All her thoughts were corralled, kept in their place, for fear of where they might go. She suppressed the troubling memories as if they had never happened. Her daily routine had become a series of small broken-down steps. Her thought processes reduced to a cartoon animation feature, a flip-book of predictable moves. And now, in a state of being high, it was curative for her to know she was capable once again of just letting her mind go. Wherever it wanted. Excluding, of course, thoughts of Warren's dying process and the funeral. She couldn't talk or think about any of *that*. Good old selective denial.

"One hour to go."

Skye was a true traveler to Vera. Her Martin. She had been for almost twenty years now, from their very first encounter. It was a nanosecond—and they both had known.

Vera couldn't remember why she had suddenly stepped forward twenty years ago at the United Way committee meeting and offered to take the picture. Perhaps it was because she hadn't said anything nice about the handmade giant cardboard check made by one of the especially needy volunteers and guilt had taken over. Whatever the reason, a photo of the committee members surrounding the big check was necessary for the next edition of the local newspaper. She had grabbed the camera from the table—took off the lens cover and aimed it at a woman she had seen around—and to her surprise, to her absolute delight, this woman, Skye, had looked directly into the camera and contorted her face. In many different amusing ways. Vera had snapped the photo, and they laughed. They both knew. Skye (in an overly serious tone) had asked Vera if she could have a copy of the picture. "I'd like to frame it for my bedside table," Skye had said.

Skye slammed the brakes—they all lurched forward and sprung back into place. Everyone screeched. "Okay ... okay! I almost didn't see the stop sign!" Skye yelled. "Relax! Jesus."

Astrid nudged Vera on the shoulder, handed her the butt end of the joint, and Vera was back in the moment.

"It's too smoky for me," Jane said, not bothering to turn her head toward Skye or Astrid, and lowered her window all the way down.

Vera was sucker punched again, with a cold roaring gust.

CHAPTER 16

THE HUT

Two may talk together under the same roof for many years, yet never really meet; and two others at first speech are old friends.

—Mary Catherwood,
Mackinac and Lake Stories

They arrived at the hut, and without unloading the car, they all went for a short stroll around part of the lake. The calm and quiet of the water reduced them to whispering. Astrid kicked a can lying on the dirt path, and they all laughed uncontrollably for what seemed like an hour. It was good stuff. Suppressing any loud laugher became the task, and it proved impossible. Astrid led the pack, her chin-length, pencil-straight blond hair swaying. Skye dawdled behind, dragging a long stick along the pathway and taking in all she could through her five senses. Astrid had warned her not to eat any mushrooms. Skye seemed unconcerned that her ankle-length skirt (woven with colorful, expensive, organic fibers) and her updated version of Birkenstock sandals were getting dirty and wet. She was that high. Jane shivered, pulling her coat up high around her neck, and complained that she was cold, so they headed for the hut.

The tiny two-bedroom hut was a square shape, with a small added rectangular offshoot for the bathroom. Vera stepped in and remembered how the pine ceilings were unusually low. It could have had a suffocating, boxlike feel to it, what with the old wooden planks surrounding her and the air damp and heavy with mustiness. But the pine wood had aged into a honey color and seemed kindly to Vera, embraced her, and she remembered that once the fireplace was lit, it would warm the room and chase the stagnant air away. The fieldstone fireplace was built to the ceiling with irregular pieces of dusky, roughened stone, massive relative to the thirty by thirty footprint of the entire hut. She had forgotten about the pine board walls and their randomly placed wormholes and knots. She smoothed her fingers over the small, rounded notches.

"How old is the hut?" asked Skye.

Astrid plunked down her worn-out backpack. "My grandfather built it for fishing in the 1920's."

Vera looked through the large picture window out to the lake. Had forgotten how close the hut was to the water.

"I hope it's heated," Jane said, her coat now pulled all the way up to her ears.

"Fireplace. What they call rustic, ladies."

"Love it. The worn oriental rugs, the mismatched furniture— it's great!" And Skye picked up her designer duffle bag. "Where do we sleep?"

"Wherever. Your choice. One has a queen bed; the other bedroom has two twins."

"Oh," Astrid said. "You should all know I'm a major snorer ..."

"I'd like one of the twin beds," Jane interrupted, in a low-pitched, steady tone. "With Skye—in the other twin bed. She is my sister-in-law. Family now …"

Jane picked up her bag, headed for the bedroom. She turned around to face them and backed away with her head bowed. "Thank you, thank you," she said with a bashful smile.

Vera felt the wormholes staring.

"Hope you brought your earplugs, Vera," Astrid said.

From Vera's angle, she could see Jane on one of the twin beds, clutching her bag, looking around the room.

Twenty minutes later, Astrid lit the fire and broke out the wine and munchies.

"My hair is frizzing up from all the dampness!" Skye said, patting down the pyramid shape. Skye could have just promenaded off the stage of a Cleopatra movie. She was always worrying about how she looked, which was ironic because Skye was stunning, with flawless enviable olive skin and a distinct, sophisticated, earthy style. Vera had never seen anyone with perfect, natural black eyeliner before she met Skye.

"So we remember … and Jane, you need to know," Astrid said. "No electronic devices. And no family talk. We don't want to leave here feeling worse than when we came. Excluding what Vera just went through, of course."

"I honestly don't want to talk about anything to do with Dad, if that's okay."

"Well, if you change your mind, we're all here for you," Skye said.

"This is so weird for me. Getting high after thirty years," Vera said.

"And why not?" Astrid said. "All the past presidents smoked pot. Think of it as being presidential. A rite of passage to greater things."

"It's great," Vera said.

"What? That they got high."

"No—changing with the times."

Vera thought of Astrid and Skye as women of the times. And they made her happy, excited her, gave her the confidence and freedom to shake things up and change, like they did. She was always a good follower when necessary.

"Ha! ... The hippie part coming full circle," Skye said.

"Yup. We were the tail end of the hippie-ness. Disco was next," Astrid said.

After the divorce from Max, Vera would sometimes say in conversation at dull events: "Yes. I was a hippie when it was fashionable. Getting high ... loved the Grateful Dead ... such beautiful harmony ... never did LSD though, you?" She could say what she wanted; she wasn't the president. She'd used the technique to simultaneously flirt and decide if further conversation was warranted. She had learned from the best, Warren, and was happy with her skill. "Ya, I was a sort of pseudo-hippie: tie-dyed and rebellious, and yet scrubbed squeaky clean," she'd say, cock her head and smile. "Whatever happened to all the peace and love?" Bat her eyelashes.

The hut warmed up and they laughed about their pseudo-hippie days: the un-scuffed hiking boots, expensive backpack, fluffy down jacket. How they'd strut about the groomed, leafy campus with an aura of carelessness as if having just woken up without a glance in any mirror, tumbled into their uniform, and wandered out the door, naturally buffed and puffed. Makeup-free beacons of truth: lovers of peace and all mankind in search of a purpose, a conviction, or a rally. But Skye talked about the tough time she had ironing out her kinky hair to make it ramrod straight, and they all agreed not having waterproof mascara available back then was a drag.

"So, Vera. Packing for Greece?" Astrid said. "So awesome."

Skye inhaled and talked through holding her breath. "Please!" she said, the word drawn out. "Stay there long enough for me to visit! ... Okay?" Exhaled a puff of smoke.

"How nice for *you*," Jane said, in an oddly exaggerated, slow-motion way.

Astrid stood, asked who was in need of more libations. "We can do cocktails too, if anyone is interested. Full bar here," she said.

Vera loved Astrid. After Vera had been fired at the college, Max told her to work somewhere that made a difference and take up a hobby. So Vera worked part-time at Planned Parenthood and continued with the oil painting. Astrid had worked for Planned Parenthood too. Hired for legal purposes but also volunteered. They had both been working the front desks: two donated oak behemoths placed side by side. Astrid seemed snotty at first. Unapproachable. Not interested in conversation and overdressed in her charcoal suit and heels. But fashionably so. The weather outside was unusually balmy for the month of November, and the protesters were out screaming in full force. The door slowly opened, and Vera had heard someone yell, "You're a murderer, and you will go to hell." The young girl faltered in. So many of the clients were young and afraid, but this girl had looked beyond scared. Vera and Astrid raced to get to her. Vera gingerly led her to a recycled church pew, and they both sat on either side of her, Astrid holding the girl's hand.

Vera couldn't remember much more about that poor, scared girl at Planned Parenthood, but her recollection of what happened between her and Astrid was so clear. They had both returned to their desks. "So, here we are," Astrid had said. "Both living the cliché of older women volunteering at PP after having kids and understanding what it takes to have one."

"I don't have any children," Vera had said softly. "I'm okay with it. You can't miss something you never had." She had surprised herself, to offer this information, this personal perspective to a stranger.

"So great to help another woman," Astrid had said, suddenly impassioned. "To see that kind of gratitude in a young woman's eyes makes you feel like a savior. Why is it that this young thing with a whole life ahead of her, be punished because she had the natural drive of someone her age to have sex and was unlucky enough to get pregnant?"

And they had looked each other in the eyes and an inexplicable bond between them had formed. It wasn't what they had said to each other that mattered, or that they were in agreement, rather how they made each other feel. A phenomenon, really. That was almost twenty years before.

Astrid held up the bottle of wine to the light of the fire. "Only one glass left of your favorite cabernet, Vera ... and last bottle too. I have plenty of other cabernets, but not this one ... so hey ..."

"Ahhhh ..." Jane interrupted. "I would like that last glass. If it's okay." She pressed her lips together in the shape of a smile and looked directly at Vera.

"Ahh ... sure, Jane," Vera said.

"I haven't had that cabernet, and I'd like to try it," Jane said.

"Sure. Go ahead."

"You're sure it's okay? I don't have to have it ... if you don't want me to."

"Sure. Go ahead," Vera said.

"Thank you. I appreciate it," Jane said, already holding out her wine glass for Astrid to fill.

Astrid emptied the bottle into the glass.

Jane gave a sweet smile to Astrid.

Astrid yanked the cork from another bottle. "I hope you like this one, Vera."

"What's everybody reading?" Skye asked. "Finished *The Elegance of the Hedgehog*. Loved it."

"Sean told me *Sozaboy* was good," Vera said. "Set in Nigeria. About being a coward."

"I love Sean," Skye said. "How is he? Oh, I brought a zucchini bread."

There was a silent lull, everybody in their own thoughts.

"I just read something about a courageous guy," Vera said, and was surprised that she wanted to do more than listen.

Jane said she wanted her warmer jacket from the car and

left. Astrid and Skye sat back and looked at Vera adoringly as if thrilled that she was talking and about to tell them a story. Damn. Like a counseling session. It was too late to drop it.

"Ya. So, it's about sati. A fucked-up ancient custom."

"Did you just say the word fuck, Vera?" Skye said.

"She needs more wine," Astrid said with a grin.

"This was way before Christianity. When a husband died, the widowed wife was expected to go along for the ride. They'd tie her up with cords in a pyre, next to her dead husband's body … and burn her alive. Some put the lucky lady into a metal cage in the shape of a body—so there was no way she could change her mind. Happened all over parts of Central and Southeast Asia. For centuries."

"Must have been a lovely bedtime read for you," Astrid said.

"So, when the British started colonizing India, people praised the dirty deed as some great religious custom not to be messed with … the natives were crazy pissed off, all up in arms, protesting to keep their Sati, said it was a time-honored tradition … blah-blah-blah. This went on for some time until finally a British officer stopped it. He said, 'My people have a custom too. When men burn women alive, we hang them.'"

There was the stoned pause of processing what had been said.

"Ideology should never trump morality," Astrid said. "But it's so hard to make a judgment call."

"Even harder to do something about it," Vera said.

CHAPTER 17

OVERRULED

The first reward of justice is the consciousness
that we are acting justly.

—Jean-Jacques Rousseau,
The Creed of a Savoyard Priest

Vera would always remember that no one ever raised her voice. Even when Astrid referred to Jane as "one of the most fucked up people I know" to Jane's face.

They all had to leave the hut and head back to Newton early Sunday morning because Jane didn't want to miss her hot yoga class. They were packed up, with only their bags, leftover food, and drinks to throw in the car—and the mood was lazy. Vera and Astrid sat together on the couch, across from Skye and Jane, in rocking chairs. There was a peaceful feeling in the hut, each woman in her own thoughts. Skye gently rocked in an unhurried, steady way. Jane rocked hard, her tempo erratic.

"I'm tired of how so many women are treated in this world," Skye said.

"Have you ever heard of vesicovaginal fistula?"

"No."

"Simply hideous." Skye grimaced. "Happens to millions of young women during childbirth in the developing world. Twelve-, thirteen-year-old girls are physically too small in size and too weak to have babies. They have tough deliveries and end up with a hole between their birth canals and rectums or bladders. Can't control their urine or shit—leaks all the time. Ends up stinking—as you can imagine. They're outcasts, even to their families."

"The answer?" Astrid asked.

"Surgery to repair the hole. Convince the parents and village elders not to marry their girls off when they are too young. Or simple contraception, if they keep their child bride traditions. Also happens to any aged woman that is in labor over two or so days."

"My God," Vera said. "Must be something besides sending money or starting an online petition."

"There is something we can all do ..." Astrid said, and sat up straight.

Jane interrupted. "Could we talk about something a little less depressing?" She grabbed the arms of her chair and straightened her spine. Stopped rocking. "I'm very upset with you right now, Vera," Jane said.

"What?" Astrid said, frowning.

"Jane ... I don't know what you're talking about." And for an instant, Vera had a sudden panicky stab of paranoia in her chest. God. What did I do?

Jane immediately bent her head down and looked to the floor, hunched her shoulders, and clasped her hands together in her lap. She gave an extraordinarily deep sigh.

"Ahh … Jane? What did I do to offend you? Did I say something … the weekend? What?" Vera asked.

Jane held her position, sat silently. Then, in a muffled voice, she said, "I feel like you ignored me at your father's funeral, Vera."

There was a hush in the hut.

Skye stopped rocking.

"You paid zero attention to me at Warren's funeral. I had an aisle seat and you looked directly at me, going in and out of the church. Then again, when you were with Sean on your way to his car. It's as if I wasn't there. I should have stayed home … you wouldn't have even noticed … really hurts."

"Wait a minute," Astrid said. "What did you just say? You think Vera was going around trying to make everybody feel special, like it was a party or something—or did it ever occur to you she was just trying to get through the fucking funeral in one piece?"

Jane redirected her stare from the floor to Vera again.

"Well … all I can say is my feelings were—and are—hurt."

Astrid contorted her face, looked at Jane sideways as Jane continued to glare at Vera.

"So, what's Vera supposed to do?"

"Well … okay. I'm sorry … so sorry for being a sensitive person. I just want Vera to know," Jane said. "That's all."

"You think she needs to hear this shit right now?"

"My feelings were—are … hurt."

"Fuck's sake. It's not all about you, Jane. Can't you put Vera's needs before your own … especially now. It's called being a humble person."

"What? I'm a very humble person," Jane said. "Ask anyone."

"Why? Because you go around all meek … and mild and you're such a good fucking listener all the time? You think that makes you humble? You hide behind your act. Like you're oh so modest. You're egocentric as hell."

Jane straightened up. "Are you guys going to let Astrid speak to me like this?"

"Leave them out of it. This is about me standing up to you—a totally fucked-up person messing with my friend."

"Nice, Astrid," Jane sneered.

And Vera said fuck you too—in her thoughts, anyway.

The car ride home was civil. Mostly, Skye and Astrid talked about what they could remember about Athens when each had separately visited for the opening of the Acropolis Museum. Gingerly asked Vera what islands she planned to visit. Jane disengaged with a continuous pout: looking down at her lap in the car and at the sidewalk all the way to the entrance of her yoga class.

A week before Vera left for Greece, she had coffee with Astrid at their favorite local café in Newton Centre. Talk revolved around how much better Vera was feeling—more like her old self—and tentative plans for Astrid to visit.

"Ya. Feeling so much better. Muddling my way back to me hasn't been easy. But I'm good. Looking forward to Greece."

"Still can't believe you got through it without any medication."

"I'm good."

"Happy for you."

"Listen. Want you to know … I think it took a lot of courage for you to say all that to Jane when we were at the hut."

"Who else was going to? You were in a fragile state of mind, and it would have been hard for Skye to say it. After all, she *is* Jane's sister-in-law now. Ouch.

"In my gut ... it was the right thing to do," Astrid said. "I've seen her pull that shit on other people before. It's all a big pity-me show. So, she gets what she wants. Selfish bitch. She manipulates with her ... what do you call it?"

"Metis," Vera said.

"She has just enough and uses it in devious self-serving ways."

"You know, Astrid," Vera said. "I've never thought of you as humble until now."

"Why? 'Cause I'm too loud and confident. Pushy?"

"You are, though. Humble. You put other people's needs before your own."

CHAPTER 18

THE PLAKA

Scratch a cynic and underneath, as often as not,
you will find a dead idealist.

—Joseph Epstein, "Our Favorite Cynic"

ike so many, she had stayed only one night in Athens before
departing to one of the islands. During the flight from Boston
Logan, Vera had considered an early morning sojourn to the
Parthenon, but in the morning, after a restless night, she opened
the shutters of her fifth-floor room to an Athens that seemed
tainted somehow. Every breath dragged heavy with dankness.
Below the window, people milled about in a colorless hue—
crushed against one another—and left no room for her. Even the
peeling building across the way, with its empty flower box, had an
unwelcome bleakness to it. There's nothing here for you, it echoed.
Everything needed a good scrub, a new beginning.

Maybe should have stayed in Kolonaki, in the square? But
then, didn't want to stay in Kolonaki—didn't want the cool crowd
either—the nice expensive hotel. This always came with the many
looks and assumptions from the well-trained staff of mostly grown

men (so openly grateful for the work), all dressed up in ill-fitting black-and-white outfits—at attention—and placed just so in their designated spots. Like polished artifacts, standing ready to assist the rich American woman. She didn't feel like being drawn into their unblinking eyes, a childlike hunger meant for boys, not for men.

No. She was not in the frame of mind for a fine hotel in Kolonaki Square. Minimum protocol here in the Plaka: no need to order, with perfect Greek elocution and flying hands, a goblet of chilled white wine with obscenely overpriced mussels and grilled ciabatta. No need for her to endlessly pick, nudge, and carefully rearrange the food into a colorful or textured pattern—never actually eating any of it. All around her, the single trendy women would be waiting, draped in folds of anticipation for the stunningly handsome man about to arrive at any moment, with a cell phone in his hand, abruptly signing off with his wife or latest mistress.

Besides, didn't have the proper shoes anymore. They were so ridiculous. The high, high heels. She could see herself stridently clicking across the hotel marble floors, clattering over the alleyway cobblestones—feeling sexy and comfortably safe from a disastrous stumble for only a few yards. Someone in Kolonaki Square would have recognized her Stella McCartneys.

Max had insisted she buy them when they were in Rome. "No animal skins, you know," Max had said. Having fallen for a pair of Jimmy Choos (definitely more foot-friendly), she had purchased the peacock blue Stella McCartneys, all the while doubting they would ever be worn. "Buy them, darling," Max had purred. "It's only a pair of shoes, for God's sake. So what if you never wear them. You'll be sorry you didn't pick them up."

They were never worn. Instead, she had carefully placed them in her closet, high above the others, where they sat perched as if in tribute to a past life with Max. The shoes could be anywhere now. Packing for Greece, she had flung them one by one across the room into a box labeled recycle.

Below the pension window, a small boy called to his father. "Baba! Perimene me!" *Dad! Wait for me!*

Warren cropped up in her mind, and with him, vague hospital images she didn't want to see. She vanquished the thoughts.

Looking out over a sprawling Athens, she suddenly had a splendid rush of optimism. It was a familiar happiness, from what seemed a long time ago. I made the right choice: Greece— and the cheap pension. And the shoes. A stripper's probably dancing around in those sexy peacock-blue shoes. Somewhere. Some club. Right now. That's where they belong. Right.

She was concerned, though, about whether the language of her casual posture, simple dress, worn, rounded shoes, and candid avoidance of cigarette smoke might be translated to those around her not as a personal choice but as rudeness. And this would never do. She could never be disrespectful to the Athenians, to the descendants of a people who had built the most magnificent monument ever to a woman. The Plaka and its boorish nature suited her right now. Even if it did boot her out of Athens early.

Didn't deliberate for long about how she would travel to the island of Naxos. Helicopters didn't go to Naxos on a regular basis and taking one of the forty-five-minute daily flights from Athens would have been the easiest way. Instead, in the cramped entrance of the pension, she inquired about the ferry.

"Kalimera," *Good morning,* she said, broadening her smile for the check-out clerk.

Without looking at Vera, the clerk's pudgy hands grabbed at the bills Vera held out.

Stumpy and sweating, the clerk had little room to maneuver in the booth behind the front desk, besides sitting on a wooden stool or standing. She stood. The cash register drawer pushed into her fleshy stomach. Roughly, she plunked the bills down, pushed the drawer back in, and turned her surly face to Vera.

"Einai sosta?" *Is that correct?* Vera asked as if speaking to a small child.

"Speak English."

"Oh. Okay."

The old woman was maybe forty years old but looked more like sixty. Her nasty stare made Vera think the clerk may have mistaken her for an opponent of some kind. She had a big, flattened nose as though someone had once whacked her with a wooden plank and this was why her crinkled face was now fully in the same plane. Her oily, matted black hair needed a good soaping. Vera guessed it was smelly too, if she got too close.

Vera tried to fight her David Foster Wallace master brain. Could the clerk not afford soap? Had the water been turned off? Did the clerk receive some bad news? Tired? Just informed she has days to live? But Vera didn't have the will to fight the master brain's default setting of self-centeredness and always seeing through her lens of self. Plus, didn't feel like working so hard to see things differently. Her lazy cynicism was winning. She was tired of always being the nice one.

Years back, when Vera had helped out at the soup kitchens, she became attached to many of the clients who were ugly and tattered and smelly. Like this woman.

Starting with a glance or a faint smile, she had developed a special rapport with many and had her favorites. Would point out a newly delivered warm coat, spoon out an extra helping of food, or sometimes just sit beside them at the tables and make small talk. They would come and go like a herd of deer. It had always been incredibly sad for her when one started to have trouble keeping up with the pack. She understood what was coming. One day, he or she wouldn't show up. Ever again.

"What do you want?"

Vera tried not to sound too chirpy, which she then did. "Oh, to karavi ... the ferry ... to ..."

The clerk sniffled. "I said English."

"Oh. You know ... cost, schedules ..." she said, sounding flat and unlike herself. Tried to make up for it with more perkiness and wide eyes.

The clerk rotated in the opposite direction from the cash register. Bent over, grabbed a ferry schedule brochure from beneath the desk, and spun it sideways onto the counter. Vera's face flushed. She picked up the brochure, felt foolish. Embarrassed. Beaten up. Look. Okay. The clerk delivered: took my money, got the ferry brochure. "What more is she supposed to do," Sally would have said. Max would have added, "Look. You're a team trying to solve an insanely complicated math equation, and your partner can't figure out the sum of two plus two. *You* are not responsible for the disastrous outcome." Right. Right.

The clerk brought her elbows to the desk, placed them together side by side, shoved her curled, chubby palms under her chin, and rested her oversized head on them. Vera thought she heard a loud fart.

"Since I'm going to Naxos ... do you know the name of their famous liqueur ... I ..."

The old woman interrupted. "Kitron," she said with a tinge of annoyance. The necessary movement of her mouth disrupted the angle of her knuckles and her perched head. She stood and sighed as if unhappy with her need to reposition. Pinched her dark eyes.

Vera winced. She smelled the strong and especially unpleasant odor of someone else's flatulence drift by.

Vera was suddenly angry, enraged: that Warren was dead, that she had traveled all this way from Newton, Massachusetts, and this was how she was greeted. Fuck you too. A fiery vision flared up of Nurse Nora, the little man and his dog Blinky. Vera abruptly turned up her nose. Raised her arm, flicked her wrist, and, with surprising force, waved the clerk away with a choppy dismissal. Don't fuck with me. Don't fuck with this queen. And was promptly ashamed that she had lost it. To be so rude and all—as if she were the center of the galaxy or something. But honestly, she knew this was the truth. She was indeed the center of not just the galaxy, but the whole universe. She fluctuated between acknowledging this truth and complete denial of this truth depending on the circumstances. In general, she chose not to believe it and propped herself up with the fallacy that she was able to view everything objectively. This untruth helped when she was in doubt, which was most of the time.

She half smiled into the clerk's dark squinting eyes. Vera lowered her eyelids to look down, stepped toward the door as casually as possible. Was still pissed off, though.

The bell on the door jingled happily as if to make up for its inhospitable, grim and cracked state of affairs. Two husky young men drifted in. One looked Asian, the other, Arab. Americans. They both smiled, first at the clerk. The clerk stared as if inanimate, a rock chiseled in the outline of a human.

The more muscular of the two, the Asian man, took off his sunglasses. "Hey," he said to her with a smile, and unloaded his backpack onto the stained concrete floor. "You all set here? Wouldn't want to cut in this long line or anything," he chuckled.

She immediately wanted to give them the heads up. Take them aside and tell them they were about to have an unpleasant time with this asshole of a clerk. Or sneak a note into one of their backpacks. Or ask them in a matter-of-fact way what two plus two equals.

As if mechanized, the clerk rotated her head around and faced the worn wooden wall of hooks and keys.

"The rooms are nice," Vera said, picking up her small red leather duffle bag. She fought with the stiffness of the unworn leather strap, slung it over her shoulder and walked out.

She hesitated to leave Athens without a visit to the Parthenon. Pay her respects to Athena and the ancient Greeks, who worshipped their extraordinary goddess for her wisdom and joy. That same amazing joy that had made Warren's death bearable, that inexplicable bond he had nurtured with travelers, who were with him in spirit as he died. She did not stay and mix with the descendants of a people who, two thousand years ago, built a glorious

monument in tribute to a woman. Ah! The impossibility of
Athens. The haunt of her ruins beneath, against the promise of
her blue sky above. But I do love Athens! And she boarded the
ferry bound for the island of Naxos.

CHAPTER 19

DEMETRI

He was like a cock who thought the sun had risen to hear him crow.

—George Eliot, *Adam Bede*

After two hours, Vera was more than ready to disembark. Greasy fumes spewed from the ferry's stack, and a cloud of black oil hung in the air. The particles quickly strayed and made their way to the ship's railing where Vera stood, holding tight. She gagged slightly and wondered what the island of Naxos would look like and how it would smell.

The air cleared to a salty clean, and from far above, the harsh wail of a soaring seagull startled her. Max once said she had beautiful hands, and they were properly attached to the right person. "That's a compliment you know, Vera," Max had said. "Always, always keep them polished." She examined one of them. Stretched and flattened her hand over the surface of the ferry railing, ran her fingers along the rough pattern of flaking rust and peeling dark-green paint. Her nails were short and polished in a subtle earthy color. Sand Dune. She decided she would let her nails go natural.

Warren had lively, lovely hands, trimmed and neat, his wrists thick from angling fish. She knew those hands intimately. The quick squeeze of that hand to secretly say, "I love you." That hand, firmly holding her tiny ten-year-old hand as he beamed with pride to formally introduce her one by one to his fishing friends, all standing in a circle around them. And those very hands, anchoring his steady grip to hold her in a hug—a pulsating hug, red with warm blood flowing—saving her, rescuing her, after Max had left for the last time. For good.

She inhaled deeply through her nose, reacted to the tingling salt in the air. She visualized a black veil sitting squarely on top of her head, draped down to her shoulders. It was the old-fashioned kind. Handmade silk lace, something an elderly Greek woman might wear to a funeral. She could feel it lift from her head, tousle her hair and free itself. She marveled at the veil's delicate needlework as it fluttered, whipped to fly, and skated across the waves—blowing soft and sometimes hard. Suddenly, it vanished. The way the pictures in her head of Warren would vanish. They'd come from nowhere. Sometimes without the attached horrific images now.

Carefully letting go of the ship's railing, she sought to gain her sea legs but still couldn't keep from teetering. Found the closest unoccupied bench, reached for it, and crashed down. On the beat-up bench across from her, a body lay curled inward. Everything was covered but the black hair. It was thick hair: too thick for a man or woman of her age. Or was it?

Loosely wrapped in a pilled and faded pink woolen blanket, the body beneath looked to have a muscular frame. The shoes were covered. This would have given it away. The covered body rustled to lie flat. Pulled the worn blanket down a bit, exposed a faint silvering at the temples. And the face. It was smooth and tight. From her angle, it was an impressive face. Chiseled, with a broadly squared chin and long straight nose; a face hinting of a bold history and a proud past, of generations filled with equally sculpted faces and the great acts of heroism one likes to imagine should correspond with such a pretty face. She wanted to touch the lovely face. Wake it up.

The face was suddenly upright, staring at her.

He laughed gently—his eyes curious and jazzed.

She hid her panic, her excitement.

"Deutsche? English? American? Ah. I hope I was not ... you know ..." He touched the tip of his nose. "How you say rochalisma? Snoring? My wife, Cora, she tell me ... snore, problem for her. Big provlima." He smiled. His teeth were perfect.

My wife? That was the end of that. This was the last thing she needed. To have an affair. Fuel the fires of scandal on the tiny island of Naxos—wouldn't take much. Oh! How islanders loved to gossip! Oh, the great sex of it all, they would chatter. Their Grecian superstar in bed with another woman. Their poor, happily married native son—tempted, seduced—ruined by the likes of the rich, bored Amerikanida. There would be the stares, the abrupt silences, the constant swirl of whispers. Shunned and scorned in person, wildly alive in the imaginations of those whom Max would have called the island "lovers of life." She would always be on top, they would fantasize.

"Can't you see it?" Max had once said to her. "Sexuality is

everywhere. It takes a lover of life to see that. To enjoy it. Don't you see it, Vera?"

She straightened her back against the bench. Suddenly felt sorry for herself.

"Amerikanida. American," she said, and sighed. "No, ochi ... you were not snoring."

This godlike specimen probably wouldn't have her anyway. Forget it.

Vera was one often swayed by physical beauty. It entrapped her. Some react to stunningly beautiful people with dismissal or jealousy. Vera would be mad to make their acquaintance. She was fully aware of this fault.

Who cares what he thinks? Who cares if he sees her as another middle-aged hag with a little too much money and nothing better to do than travel around the world trying to find herself (after extensive volunteering and fundraising in the homeland didn't do the trick). Probably as stupid as a tree stump.

She looked closely into his eyes and searched. Recognized it at once—the familiarity, the delight of having found such a prize within human eyes. It was immediate—the clarity—and a different kind of magic flared. They were a match: he had the makings of a likely friend for her. Perhaps a traveler. She could see he could see this. He would know what makes a traveler.

"... you travel karavi ... ferry ... before?" he asked, his voice husky and smooth, unraveling before her with the ease of a silvery ribbon.

"Not this one."

"Ah ... benches hard," he said. "Harder and harder—every

time." He smiled. They both laughed. Knowingly.

"My Anglika, okay? Okay to speak my English? I need the exaskisi, need practice," he said.

He spread his arms wide. "Etsi katalavo tis eidisesis tou kosmou." *That way I understand the news of the world.*

She had no idea what he said (well … she did know the word *news*). Fumbling with her cell phone, she searched for the needed words. "Fysika!" *Of course.* "And only if I may speak to you in Greek … Ellinika."

She expected this would not last long. And it didn't. He had a much better command of English than she had of Greek; English happened. She was lazy. He got his way.

"My name Demetri. I am agrotis." *farmer.*

"Vera Mine." Bowed her head slightly. Tapped her cell. "Eimai apo tin America … was teacher, psychologia …" *I am from the States. Taught psychology.* She left out the part that she was essentially fired.

"Ach."

"Have you lived on Naxos long?"

"My oikogeneia … family … how you say? … Forever … periousia … land … handed down."

She glanced at her cell for the translation. "Generations," she said.

She could barely contain herself. This simply could not be happening. God damn! It was this metis thing. Demetri. It was all beyond coincidence. Steaming ahead on Grecian waters, having just left the Parthenon and her beloved goddess Athena, the symbol of metis. There was no doubt. Demetri had metis. Maybe major metis.

"Nai. Yes, gen ... eration. You stay here ... Naxos long?" The perfect teeth flashed again.

"Pou tha meinete?" he asked.

Vera immediately monkeyed with her cell phone.

"Where you stay?" he said, with a wide, warm grin.

"Rented a cottage near the Finikas Hotel. Pyrgaki Beach ..."

"Ochi! I live in Pyrgaki."

"On the beach?"

"Piso! Behind the hotel. Ah ... no kalliergo ... special Greek patates!" *I cannot grow my special Greek potatoes on a beach!* And Demetri raised his right arm, kissed his thumb and forefingers, shook them at eye level. "Ahhh ... den boro na fytepso stin ammo." He laughed. *Can't plant in the sand.*

"You stay at Makris Cottages?" he asked.

"Nai ... yes."

"Ach ... you be happy. They nice." Nodding his head. "I like you to meet my oikogeneia ... family. Nai?"

"Love to." She flushed.

"My wife—good cook. I tell her to make pastitsio. My wife will cook you ..."

"Your wife will cook me?"

"Ach ... say to ... you ... silly things in English." Demetri paused. Appeared wounded.

"No worries if you do...."

A spirited wind from the sea silenced them. They both raised their chins, caught the pleasure from its coolness. A black backpack on Demetri's lap caught her eye. It looked new, expensive. This is what he must have been curled around when he was sleeping.

He eyed her red leather travel bag. "You ypologisti ... computer ... yes?"

"Hard to be without one ..."

"Ach ..." he broke off, paused.

"Andras ... husband?"

"Yes. He died over two years ago, but we were divorced before ..."

"Ach."

Slightly rattled, her eyes darted downward. "Yes. Max and I were married for many years."

What she wanted to say was ... Max divorced her for a stereotypical trophy wife, twenty years his junior. You see, Max was always able to see the sexuality in everything around him ... he died of a brain aneurism in her arms: he died in the sex-kitten's arms. After they fished him from the pool.

Quietly, she looked up and added, "A few regrets."

Right. She certainly wasn't going to get into translating the word regrets. She toyed with the idea Demetri would someday learn everything about her. Oh ya. She'd take him if he'd have her. Fuck the natives.

"... But it was my father. He died about a year ago. He's the one I'm getting over. Not Max. Got over him a long time ago." She doubted Demetri caught all of this.

"Sorry. About pateras...." *father....*

Shifting her attention to the backpack held upright in his lap, she asked, "You go to Athens, the mainland, a lot?"

"Nai. Once week." His fingers ra-ta-tap the backpack. "Our government give us ... all agrotes, farmers ... new laptops." Carefully, he laid the backpack flat on his lap.

"Oh?"

"Yes. Agrotes today businessman too. Have to, to survive!" He laughed in a forced, guttural way.

"Has the EU affected your business greatly?"

"Middlemen, private food companies, okay. Government used to help us ... agrotes in bad times. Now, with troika ..." Demetri shook his head from side to side. "Now, different. All they do is raise taxes ... on us. Poor agrotes."

"Troika?"

Demetri scoffed. "Greek creditors—European Commission, European Central ... how you say ... Bank? IMF. Ta tria diavoloi ... the three devils."

"Wow. Your English is quite good."

"Need to keep up with what devils do to ... us." And shook his head.

"Are your trips to Athens every week related to the agrotes? Didn't I read somewhere about farmers driving their tractors—like over three hundred tractors ... to the center of Athens—Nikaia? To blockade roads?"

Demetri nodded, yes. His eyes locked on hers.

"You were there today? To protest in Nikaia?"

"I have business in Exarcheia."

"Exarcheia?"

Demetri was taken aback. "Ah. You think you know Athens?" he said, suddenly serious and stern. "Greek business everywhere." He lightened up with a smile, said, "Even in Exarcheia there is Greek business."

Still, she was surprised by this. Exarcheia was well known

as a center for Greek anarchists.

The ferry was coming into port.

"My wife, my children, they wait … for me. I want you meet them … Ver-a."

It was the first time she had heard him say her name. His deep voice played with her two-syllable name, gave it a heavenly, yet seductive cadence.

With his backpack tucked under one arm, Demetri pointed them out to her from the ferry. The wife held the shoulders of two children, one on each side, a boy and a girl. They looked happy enough. The children appeared to be about the same age, eleven or so. They stood together with another man in front of a rusted and beat-up powder-blue truck.

"Are your children twins, Demetri?"

"Yes! Like a day and a night." He laughed. She needed to cock her head back and look up to him. He was way over six feet. His dark jeans were tight. His white shirt tucked in. Wow. Farmers wear white shirts?

Demetri's wife looked pleasant. There was a gauntness and frailty about her from a distance, as if she had to clutch the shoulders of both her twins for support or she would fall. It was a lopsided affair. The girl was the tallest. The mother let go of her, and the boy and his mother seemed to wave in unison at the big boat. The girl, standing on her own, arms at her sides, searched the decks, looking. Demetri wildly motioned with his arms, and the girl, having found her father, waved back with glee. It was unmistakable. Demetri and his daughter waved solely to each other.

Demetri's white van was being repaired. His friend, Christos, the man with the light blue truck, was waiting to drive his family back to Pyrgaki. Demetri told her that he wouldn't want her to ride in the dirty old truck.

"Island small. I see you," he said, and sprinted ahead of her.

She disembarked alone. The lines were long, moved slowly. The docked ferry gunned and blared the ready engines, soaking the air around her with the foul smell and taste of diesel. An edginess took hold, and she started to doubt: felt truth was hiding from her. Her decision to be in Greece was based solely on her perspective as "queen of the universe." It had been an emotional, biased decision. There was nothing objective or practical about her being here, on this ferry. She tried to not fully breathe in the air. Calmed herself with the idea that her friends agreed she should move to Naxos. They had looked carefully at the facts and had made an informed decision. Vera went with this last thought and took a step. She lifted the leather strap of her bag over her head and across her chest. And Vera stepped onto the land, into the village, and directly into her soul.

She startled at the color. True color as it was meant to be— so simply blue, so simply white—yet brilliantly complex from an effortless juxtaposition. The scrubbed steps beckoned to her, their steep up and down alleyways of bleached white stucco echoed a soothing rhythmic pulse with each step. She flirted with the choices, seemed to dance along the narrow winding ways of the jumbled and twisting curves. She looked up. The great sheath of a cloudless blue called and drew her in, delighted her, with a mirror of the sparkling sea: a vast ocean, so true, so deep, so heavy with teeming life that she was suddenly struck with an urge to jump into the salty water—live the hues of life—be a part of it. My God! Like nowhere else in the world, had blue against white so touched her.

CHAPTER 20

THE COTTAGE

Arrange whatever pieces come your way.

—Virginia Woolf, *A Writer's Diary*

Vera felt every bump. The taxi drive to the Pyrgaki Beach area turned out to be a half-an-hour ride, and she was tensed up, couldn't seem to relax—kept trying to keep herself still—so when she discovered her rented cottage to be delightful, her sense of relief was all the more poignant. It was perfect.

Private. And so quaint: a string of small sugar-cubed cottages with blue painted doors slightly peeling, all braided together with a rickety white arbor. The arbor was slightly cockeyed—overflowing, dripping—with tiny petals of pink bougainvillea and blooms of brightest white jasmine. She closed her eyes to breathe in the warm, syrupy fragrance. Felt welcomed. The God-awful bumps, the putrid smell of the ferry's diesel fumes seemed a lifetime ago.

Her unit was at the end. The enclosed back terrace was open to the sky, and as Vera looked up, she imagined herself there in the still silence of nighttime: pitch-black darkness strewn with tiny flickerings, telling her, reassuring her of fate. All she needed to do was be here. Be present. Live all this. Fate would take care of the rest. And she hoped to keep this frame of mind for as long as possible.

She looked at the bushy orange tree standing at attention in the corner of her terrace. Noted its unwieldy limbs and shaggy leaves: perfect for daytime shade. The tree was laden with fruit, and she had heard that the oranges in Greece were slightly bitter. She hoped these would be the exception.

A centuries-old marble floor lay beneath four white plastic chairs gathered around an unsteady wooden table, a plastic blue-and-white checkered tablecloth thumbtacked around its edges. A faded terra-cotta bowl sat in the center of the round table, holding bold, bright-red geraniums—needed water.

She found a warm bottle of water on a shelf and a frosted, old-fashioned metal ice tray in the top freezer of the tiny refrigerator. Cooled herself off with a tall glass of water and listened for the crackling ice as she sat at her patio table for the first time. What do you think, Dad? Vera was becoming more and more successful at separating thoughts of Warren from any raw images.

Her thoughts wandered to the beach, only a five-minute sashay. And a schedule: paint early morning; nap; read; and, later in the day, amble to the beach for inspiration. Repeat.

This was perfect for Vera, as she was never much of a daytime beach person. Never cared for the heat and burn of a midday sun. Nor the hordes. She would show up all bubbly, wearing her tied shoes and long pants, or a long flowing skirt, while everyone else, practically naked and sapped, was leaving the beach in droves. She liked the idea that those she passed on her way, thought she was going in the wrong direction at the wrong time.

Never cared much for the beach sand either. To her, each pebble of sand was a mean little pointed fellow who, with glee, scraped and irritated, interfered with the whole reason to be there—the sights and sounds, the salty smells, the overall intoxication.

Once, long ago, on Crane's Beach in Massachusetts, Vera remembered she had tried to save the day, stop a little girl's water toy from venturing out to sea. The water was only fifty-seven degrees, and Vera had plunged into the agonizing rush of the sudden cold immersion. It had been a failed rescue; they stood on the beach and waved goodbye to the blown-up pink tiger as it floated out of sight. The girl had cried, rubbed her eyes, and got sand in them. Cried harder.

Vera plunked down the glass, the remaining ice cubes bobbed.

One more example of when she had needed Goddamn Max. He was the stronger swimmer. Where the hell had he been? Off to socialize with the cool young beach crowd? Damn the sand. And damn Max. And Vera shifted from the continuation of yet another rumination that blamed Max for something he had nothing to do with, and she had a flutter of triumph.

God, Dad. It's good I'm here. Right? Right.

Heard a gentle knocking on her cottage door. It was five o'clock in the afternoon.

Before she could fully open the wide, weather-beaten door, a little girl announced, "Sas fernoume stifado me fasolia kai tomates!" Then in English she said: "We're bringing you bean and tomato stew! For you!"

Within hours of Vera's arrival, Demetri's wife and the twins had come to visit her.

"Kalos orisate!" *Welcome!* they said, or the girl said, and the other two mouthed the words.

They all smiled modestly. The boy looked down at his humdrum dirty white sneakers. The bony mother bobbed her head, hands covering her mouth, and looked at Vera sideways as if sneaking a peek. The nails looked bitten; the flesh of her fingers sore. The girl held both handles of the round pot with two ragged potholders, waited until Vera looked her in the eyes, and straightened her little arms out and up to show Vera the pot.

"It means welcome. You like? Favorite in whole world."

"You speak English!"

"We learn English in school from first grade," the girl said, giving the kitchen a once over.

"Smells delicious! Please, come in," said Vera, holding open the door. A few cornflower-blue paint chips fell to the marble step.

The girl walked in. Her mother and brother followed to the corner of the tiny kitchen. With some effort, the girl heaved up the beat-up tin pot and slid it onto the linoleum countertop.

The boy whispered into his mother's ear. The mother shook her head, cupped a hand to cover her mouth.

"I explained to her. We are invited to come in," he said to his sister, in a surprisingly high-pitched and melodious voice. Excellent. He spoke English too.

The girl pointed to her mother and brother. "Cora. Tasso." In a louder and clearer voice, she said, "Me, Elektra."

"Vera." She pointed to herself.

The black center knob of the lid was cracked in half. Lifting it, Vera remarked: "The stew smells wonderful," and she turned to see Tasso eyeing her. He looked down.

Elektra said, "O Tassos mazevi kremmydia simera. Eklepsa ta pio oraia kai ta'vaza sto stifado." *Tasso bagging onions today. I stole three nice ones and put them in the stew.*

Vera picked up on the word for onion: kremmydia. Onions were somewhere, doing something.

Cora's skittishness seemed to come and go. Vera spotted worry in Cora's eyes: palest brown in color, translucent—yet somehow dense. Cora's worry seemed unfocused, inward. The eyes were set far apart and gave her that dumb look. But they were kind. What could Cora be worried about: That Vera would surely fuck her husband until he was senseless? The islanders would gossip about her, and tell her that Vera was always on top?

The slow creep of self-disgust consumed Vera for a second. God. Truly incorrigible. Or, maybe she was beginning to see the sex everywhere around her.

Vera smiled at Cora so long and hard that the corners of her mouth hurt. Went on to tell them they were so kind. "Eiste toso … evgenikoi." This was a line she had been practicing, and she looked for their reactions. Tasso and Cora looked their separate ways, and from Elektra's eyes, it was clear Vera's execution had been pathetic.

The twins were not identical. Far from it. Elektra's fleshy frame gave the illusion that Tasso was small, even though he was probably average for his age. Elektra was blessed with a physical beauty usually reserved for the fantasies people might have about famous actors—her light olive complexion was flawless. Her teeth brightest white. She was the spitting image of her father.

Vera ceremoniously held out her arm toward the terrace. "Come."

Elektra skipped out and slid onto a chair. Tasso guided his mother with short, even steps.

"Water?" asked Vera.

"Do you have ice?" Elektra said with the energy of a bouncing ball.

Tasso and his mother shook their heads no, and Vera couldn't help but think they were denying an evil deed or something. Tasso's thin shoulder-length hair was barely anchored behind his ears. She wanted to tie his hair back in a low ponytail.

There was a knock on the door. It was a hard knock, but rhythmic, sounded friendly.

Another guest! The knock seemed to jolt, shock her company a bit. She sensed a new worry from Cora and excitement from Elektra. Tasso didn't react. He glanced at Vera, abruptly looked away.

From the terrace, she could see through the crack of the door that they'd left ajar. It was Demetri! He did not wait for her. He strode in. And this was fine with perpetually private Vera, who would have been appalled at the rude presumptuousness of opening a partially closed door without an invitation to do so. Perhaps it was her great mood, her sudden sense of delight upon seeing him again, or perhaps it was because she was finally feeling a bit more like herself for the first time since Warren died (eight weeks ago now) and she was back—but better. She stood from her plastic chair. He extended his hand. She grabbed it, attempted to give a strong handshake, but it came across as a prolonged squeeze.

Elektra flew into her father's outstretched arms. His thick wrists and bear-paw hands pulled Elektra's petite head against his brawny chest, and he cradled, gently patted, and smoothed her hair. He kissed the top of her head.

Tasso and Cora remained seated. Cora leaned slightly forward at the waist with her arms crossed. Her breasts were enormous for her petite size. They gave her an innocent dowdiness and Vera imagined them as soft and warm but reminded herself that they belonged to Demetri's roughened hands. Sitting right there, before her, was the official, legal wife. Right. —Right. Cora continued nodding for a while. Tasso sat back with what appeared to be virile confidence, but the gesture was exaggerated and seemed phony to Vera.

Demetri's appearance energized everyone and everything on her terrace. The earth seemed to alter its angle for the sun to give them all more shade. A perfumed puff from the jasmine flowers wafted by and lingered. Somehow the geranium glowed a brighter red. Vera half expected a ripened orange to fall from the tree.

Tasso suddenly stood. His eyes were wildly alert yet controlled. His jeans were clean—too long and too baggy—his T-shirt too wide; if caught in a strong gust of wind, he could flap and sail away. There was a reticence about him—a young John Lennon without the wire-rimmed glasses. Tasso did not look like farmer material.

"Baba," Tasso said. *Dad*, "I need to leave now. Haven't bagged the onions yet. I know you wanted them bagged today and ..."

"You already bagged them today!" Elektra interrupted.

Demetri ignored Elektra and turned his gaze to Tasso. "Good.

Okay, to leave," he said, and sat up straighter. Pushed his mighty shoulders up and back.

Tasso stared, as if to study Demetri's face. "Okay, Baba." Tasso nodded to his mother and Vera, began to walk from the terrace with heavy steps that seemed overdone.

Demetri raised his mighty arm. "Ahhh … Tasso. Take your mother home too." And dipped his chin once, as if to signal, you can go now.

Cora jumped up, clumsily caught up with Tasso, and he dropped back behind her.

Demetri scanned from Vera to Elektra and back as if weighing the situation with the new configuration of three. Placed his hands behind his head. His lips were slightly parted. Wet.

Cora's empty chair had a cracked, wobbly leg … she'd talk with Antonio, the rental manager … Vera had a feeling she'd be staying in Naxos for a while.

You were right, Dad … no need to put my stuff in storage.

Miss you so much.

CHAPTER 21

WARREN RETURNS

Sad is this continual postponement of life.

—Ralph Waldo Emerson

"**M**agnificent?"

"Yes. Magnificent," Vera said, talking on her cell phone.

"Hon. I don't think I've ever heard you use that word."

"Firsts with you always feel right, Sean."

"Seriously? Things are magnificent?" Sean howled.

"Yes," she paused. "Yes, yes, they are."

"You mean fucking magnificent, right, hon?" Sean said, and she imagined his wry grin. "Use all your new words now, Vera. You're lucky I'm up this early," he said.

"I've been in Greece twenty-eight days now. When are you coming?"

"No. twenty-nine. How's the cuisine?"

"So far, I've learned that the finest, freshest salads in the world don't need any lettuce at all, and fried red snapper is pretty good."

It had been three months since Warren died, and here she was.

Sitting on her terrace at two in the afternoon Greek time, talking with her best friend.

She had initiated the call to Boston. Sean never called anyone. He liked this, being pursued. She had asked him about it many times, angrily once, over coffee at their favorite coffee bar, looking for a simple explanation as to why he never, ever called her first.

"Why do I always have to call you, damn it, Sean! What's your problem?" She remembered he had been perplexed by her irritation, seeming almost hurt at first, wanting to know what was so terribly awful about wanting to be the one unequivocally chosen. Desired, preferred above all the rest.

"I'm just one of many, Vera, from all the great fields of flowers," he had said. "And this flower prefers to be, is happiest, when rooted—I hope you're writing this all down, Vera. Yes, this little flower is happiest when fastened to the lushness of its soil, tiny white tendrils of life—so tenuous—reaching down to nest, to burrow, to bed tidily and safely within the warmth of a dark, rich loam."

She had interrupted, "Sounds like an insecure homebody to me ... not a flower."

He had looked at her sternly, up and away. "I'm not finished yet, Vera. And this poor flower, this mostly happy, teensy, rooted flower, can only wait. Wait to be lopped off from its root, wait to be plunged into ice-cold water, only to wait again, with great hope: to be noticed and desired, to be chosen and cherished as a single stem—yet knowing, always knowing that it could be mixed with others at any moment in a hideous, squabbling bouquet."

Sean had sighed, long and hard. "Goddamn!" he had yelped.

"No wonder the little flower needs antianxiety meds!"

"Seriously, Sean, you need to see someone. It's time. You're not a flower. And there's no reason why you can't call me, text me, FaceTime me, even write me *first*—for God's sake!"

"Easy for you to say. You're not so much a flower ... as a picker," Sean had told her.

This was true. She had a thing about flowers and was never one to purchase a ready-made bouquet (unless last-minute desperate) or leave it up to the florist, so eager to dispose of the unwanted. She was a picker. She recognized that slight wink from the florist, with a nod as if to say, we'll take good care of you—followed up with a quick wisp of the hands—and Vera would be ushered out the door with dying inventory. A bunch of boring daylilies or, worse yet, pink-and-blue-dyed carnations, concealed beneath one or two sublime specimens. Such a waste of time! she would say to herself, as she tossed the unwanted stems down the disposal. Ground them up good.

She preferred to do her own picking and choosing. She knew what she wanted. She would click open the flower-shop door and, at first, simply delight in the sights and smells of all the flowers together. But to take a few flowers home with her, this was another matter. Each flower suddenly became individual—one predictably boring, one uniquely bent this way or that, one clearly trying to hide from her. For the most part, many were not worth her effort, not worth her tender care, not so pleasing.

In the business, she became a legendary customer. One who demanded time from the salesclerks. Respectful, they'd have to shuffle around and around with her as she pointed to this flower and that. With her careful direction, stunning bouquets were gathered. "Is she a bitch, or just particular?" the florists would say about her after she snapped the shop door shut. "I don't know. But she does have an eye for it."

She heard Sean breathe into the cell phone.

"Are you listening? Well, isn't this a big change? Me asking you this question … why haven't I heard from you?" he said.

"Been busy."

"I suppose all your new little Greek friends have scurried off for nap time, so being bored, you called little ole me? I'm so flattered."

"You should be. Very busy."

"Busy with what, with whom, hon? I want to know everything. I miss you so much, Vera."

"Couple of new friends."

"And who are you schtupping, if I may ask? That's what I wanna hear about. Shagging, screwing, whatever you want to call it."

She laughed. "I'm not schtupping anyone!"

"Then how can everything be so damn magnificent!"

This was always open to debate between them. Sean's position was that sex should be a part of one's life until one's demise. He would rave over and over about a successful penile implant on a ninety-three-year-old and seem genuinely concerned that Vera didn't fully appreciate and marvel at this new medical breakthrough.

"I don't need sex the way you do, Sean," Vera would say. "Been there, done that. I'm more interested in other things now."

"Please … call a sex therapist. You know … for the malady … the opposite of sexual addiction," Sean would say.

"Sex? Much rather paint, see a play, pay a complete stranger for a good massage. I'm not the fucked-up one, you know. You are, Sean. Needs change."

"Christ!" Sean would roar. "You're only fifty-five! Are you going to go thirty years without sex?"

"Besides. Whatever happened to the words make love?"

Hormonally, Vera acknowledged she was a mess. Had talked about it openly. Once, she had shared with Astrid and Skye how she could not stop herself from equating old people publicly caressing each other (well, over eighty anyhow) with attention-starved teenagers—green streaked hair, tightly wrapped in black leather and chains. This seemed out of whack to her. Old people making out in public, being overtly sexual. Like a gnarly old woman chewing bubble gum and playing with a slingshot or a five-year-old asking who you're voting for. Astrid and Skye had only listened.

She switched her cell phone to speaker. Laid it on the plastic checkered tablecloth. Noticed the blue-and-white checks were fading on the edges a bit. The metal thumbtacks rusty.

"Okay. Well, tell me when you finally do. Schtup, shag, whatever you want to call it. Make love. They're not mutually exclusive, you know."

"Fine. Whatever. I'd love to be with this one guy.…" And she stared at a thumbtack that was out of line.

But she was not. And the reason had more to do with Vera's will (and Demetri's will too—she respected him for this). She had to control the default setting of thinking only of herself on just about a daily basis. Especially when Demetri deliberately teased with the provocative, slow blink of his eyelashes—especially when she could see he was feeling weak too. But she always chose not to give in to instant gratification and the best sex she quite possibly could ever have. She and Demetri were good friends. Lovers, perhaps in a fantastical, private, dreamy way. It was more than a romantic love; a love of the finest kind, a love based on trust, mutual enjoyment. She would often remind herself that taking him would blur, destroy, the carnal fantasies she had of them entangled: there on the terrace, in her bed, in the potato fields.

"A guy, did you say? Traveler or metis? I get them mixed up," Sean said into his cell phone.

"They're related, dummy."

"Oh, yes, that's right," Sean said with exaggerated articulation and seriousness. "Vera, you are a prude. Plain and simple," he said.

"I'm not a prude, Sean," she said with surprising force. Bit her lip.

"Get with the times."

"Well, S-e-a-nnnn. You probably aren't aware of this, but age is a consideration when changing with the times."

"Let me guess. While everybody else cruises the beach naked, looking for action, you're showing up with a cardigan sweater draped over your shoulders, attached at the neck with your gigantic pink cameo pin."

"Not true, Sean. I didn't even pack my cameo."

"No!"

"Yes. And I would gladly be schtupping my Demetri, but he's married. With kids."

"I feel a lecture coming on."

"What can I say? We can't all be as lucky as you and Johnnie."

"How so?" Sean asked.

"We can't all have a true, noble love—and great sex."

There was a pause.

"Johnnie says hello. He knows how much I miss you. I talk about you all the time, you know. Vera this, Vera that."

"So. Will you be visiting me soon? You said you would, Sean."

"Yes. Love to. Maybe over Johnnie's next school break. I think he'll be busy with private tutoring—so maybe then. He's all good. Teaching a new graduate course—embedded computation. Likes the class makeup."

"I need dates."

"How's the painting? And don't say it's magnificent. Please."

"Okay. I won't. But it's fantastic."

"Gotta go. I miss you, hon. Ciao."

Vera clicked her cell phone off and continued to sit on her terrace, zeroed in on the veins of a leaf hanging from the orange tree, sketched it out in her mind. At three o'clock in the afternoon, the air was hot, and she tried to imagine a fleeting cool breeze. Uncomfortable with the heat, she touched the arm of her chair, fingered the molded plastic, so hard and unforgiving; she managed to find a soft comfort—her fingers repositioned the small needlepoint pillow with the word love on it, tucked it into the curve of her back (the cushion Max had given her). Barefoot, she scuffed the soles of her feet slowly and tenderly across the warm shaded marble beneath. And yes, it was all magnificent. Especially, and most importantly, because of her art.

The last month had been a never-ending sweet indulgence, with flowing associations and perfect strokes of paint. A mere touch here or a smell there triggered a clear direction for her. She hardly slept. But when she did, each night astonished: dreams of classical paintings and sculptures of powerful gods gone mad. Masculine gods: Dionysus and his reckless gaiety and stupors; Antaeus's murderous rampages on innocent trekkers; the cruelty of Zeus's infidelities. Usually, in the end, the wise and courageous goddess Athena would step in to save the world from this brutish mania—only to be raped by Hephaestus. But she would fight him off, his sperm would scatter to the earth and produce a son, whom Athena would adopt as her own. Once, the son looked like Tasso. Another time, David Bowie.

The imaginative nights gave way to luminous mornings and long, productive days. She was energetic, happy, and creative. She painted like mad.

Yet it was a new painting experience. She already had the technical skills: the precision. Knowing what brush to use, how to execute the shapes and forms from a charcoal sketch, how to add depth and texture with minute levels of paint thickness. How to leave the painting to dry for days, sometimes weeks, returning to paint exactly what she wanted in shading, color saturations, and shadows—many times painting over what she had already done. But here, now, in Greece, it was different. Her painting had transformed from simple skill to having a voice, her paintings now spoke for her—with originality and risk. Her work was honest. Exhilarating.

Vera stood outside of the orange tree's shade and caught the silhouette of her shadow on the parched marble—lithe and graceful. She had lost weight, surely.

Yes. It was all magnificent. Mostly because of the recent surprise images of Warren—the old images pushing out the most recent unpleasant ones. Without reason or pattern, he was suddenly there, and Vera so completely trusted the images of him that her lovely, remembered emotions attached to the imagery felt real. He would come to her in portrait mode: torso up, looking healthy with his cheeks rosy and full. He was always thrilled to see her— his wise eyes and kind smile telling her so. It was a happy place to be. She alone had his full attention. He was all hers.

She heard a knock.

Demetri let himself in. Came toward her.

CHAPTER 22

POLITICS, CHOCOLATES, AND SEX

Imagination is a very high sort of seeing.

—Ralph Waldo Emerson, "The Poet"

The burn on the soles of her feet sizzled and shimmied up the backs of her legs as she popped her feet into the leather flip-flops. It was the following day, and Vera was sitting on the terrace talking on the phone with Sean again about his upcoming trip.

"Really can't wait to see you, hon," Sean said.

"Same," said Vera.

"Any updates on the sexual situation?"

"Stop it."

"Well, I've been thinking, and I'm just going to put this out there … maybe you have vaginal atrophy."

"Seriously? You're the one who needs to see a few sex therapists. Ever heard of the affliction … Addiction to Sexual Thoughts?"

"Must be something new. Just trying to help. Anyway, I have a close friend who takes some kind of a concoction to increase her estrogen."

"What friend?"

"Astrid."

"What! Astrid! Why hasn't she told *me* this!"

"Because you and she disagree about this subject. Generally. How else do you think she struts around like a goddess in heat? And why do you think she never helped you with your idea about 'Say No to Sex' rally?" Sean said. "I'm sure she won't mind that I told you, but just in case, don't tell her I told you."

"I'll tell Astrid whatever I want. It's a really good thing for you—that I do love you," Vera laughed.

She sighed into the cell phone as deeply, as loudly, and for as long as possible.

"Okay. Okay … so anyway …" Sean said.

She looked up to see Demetri standing in the kitchen again. He had let himself in. He swaggered toward her.

"Sean. Sorry to interrupt. I have a visitor."

"Fine. Fine. Can't wait to see you though! Ciao." Sean clicked off.

She settled back in her plastic chair. Ah—Demetri. A shaft of the sun's light shifted and bent to shine only on him. She squinted, could practically see the tiny floating particles shift into slow-motion. In her mind, the haze around Demetri turned golden and, with a mighty sickle in his hands, he scythed his way through the harvest toward her—the hay, waist high and prickly, bending and rippling with his every step. She touched. Slowly ran her finger along the curved edge of the blade, razor-sharp, and, for a second, was slightly afraid of it, of him. Honest to God. She would do anything. Anything for her Demetri.

"Hey." He smiled.

"Hey."

"Hey, you," Demetri mouthed in a whisper. "I have surprise for you." He seemed buoyant.

He placed a white cardboard box on the plastic blue-checkered tablecloth. On top of the box lay a purple flower with a bright-yellow center, held in place with gold elastic, tied in a small bow. Noticed he did not have his computer with him, again. Carefully, with both hands, Demetri picked up her laptop and placed it where he would sit. He re-cupped the gift box in his hands as if it were an offering, and, in one majestic swoop, arranged it squarely on the table in front of her. He settled down on his chair, flipped open her computer.

"Oh. So lovely!"

Demetri smiled.

Everything in Greece was wrapped up. Cutely decorated. Even the fish market had a special paper and colorful cord to dress up the squid and sardines carted home each week for deep frying with onions in native olive oil. She pretended the wrapping was more exceptional to her than it was.

"So pretty! May I guess?" Vera chirped. "Chocolates?"

"Ahhhh ... Sokolatakia for you. Vera."

Her thighs were sticky with sweat, and she pushed her cotton dress down between her legs. Demetri and her computer were in the shade, and she shimmied her plastic chair from the partial sun, moved closer to him, pushed against the needlepoint pillow at her back.

"Have you paint much for today?" he asked, touched the side of his handsome nose.

"A little. But it's good."

"Good is what matters."

They both looked away, stared at the purple flower on top of the box, mesmerized by the velvety petals. The flower's deep color and texture spoke, begged them to touch and see if it could feel as beautiful as it looked. But they did not. It was understood that she would open the box and eat the sweets later. She would touch the tiny flower when she was alone. She pushed the box into the shade.

"Ah, you see, I forget my computer."

"Demetri!"

His eyes darted back and forth to the computer; he seemed embarrassed.

"Go ahead. Use mine," she said.

He threw his head back, laughed. She honestly had never seen such glistening white teeth.

"… Na kytaxo to email mou simera … check my mail today." And he logged on.

Vera had used the words "Yankee ingenuity" once with Demetri when discussing the origins of the computer, and as soon as she said it, she conceded how obsolete the phrase was. Offensive now to some people, she guessed. She hadn't bothered trying to explain it to him. They both could see it, anyway—they too, like the phrase, were obsolete, at least technologically. And they bonded over this: became computer companions, a duo, nascent computer aficionados with a mission—sharing their computer questions, computer knowledge, and first encounters.

It became routine. Demetri visited late morning, well after she had been most productive (she was up at five now, to bed at midnight or later, on Greek time). And together, in the shade, with their computers (on the days he could remember to bring his), they would work opposite one another, catching up on the news, checking mail.

"You are so sweet to bring me these chocolates!"

Demetri looked up from reading his email. His mood had changed.

"Everything okay?"

"Yes. Yes. I … how to say? Frustrate. Apogoitevmenos!"

"EU again?"

Demetri appeared more angry than frustrated. She had boned up on what was happening with the Greek farmer—enough to have a meaningful conversation with him about it. This topic was important to him, and she was roused, liked it, whenever he got emotional—about anything.

"Ahhhh … government now want to up tax on agrotes!"

She sat back in her chair to get comfortable. Listened. Noticed the perfect curve of his dark eyebrows. As if he had spent hours in front of a mirror plucking them.

"Diavoloi devils want to up my taxes, down my tax breaks— cut pensions!" Demetri threw both hands up.

"Well …" she said, startled by the swing in her tone to serious business. "This is the third bailout for Greece. They owe billions of dollars—you know. They have to make some reforms. Somewhere."

"Why us! Always agrotis—farmer!"

Shaking her head in agreement, she was captivated by his increasing intensity. "Well … you do know …" she said, "not all Greek people support you. Some think of you as a pampered group who, since the financial collapse in '08, have had tax breaks and subsidies for decades while everybody else has had to make sacrifices."

"Devils—no pensions for any us! Crazy!"

Unhurriedly, she raised her right hand up, ready to gesture with it, and replied, "Well … the lenders want their money … and say farmers should be treated like any other professional businessmen."

"So? Don't pay back! Greek people be fine!"

"Gee … I don't know.… If you don't follow through on your agreement with the creditors, Greece may be in danger of leaving the EU."

"Good. They make only misery for us!"

She raised her left hand up and tilted her head toward it. "Well, Demetri. If you leave the EU, domestic inflation will sky- rocket. Prices of imports will skyrocket too—and you import practically all of your necessities."

"We need stand up. Get out of EU. Go back to the way things were! They want to change our culture."

Vera's face flushed. She leaned toward him. "Well … who do you think is going to be hit hardest if you pull out of the EU? Farmers and poor people … they are the ones who won't be able to pay for even the most basic things, like food, medicine, petrol."

Demetri turned from her, glowered at the computer screen.

"Anyway, seems as if the Greeks are always in the streets protest- ing something or other. Maybe it's a cultural thing or genetic," Vera said, and immediately worried she might have sounded patronizing.

"You don't know."

She gazed at him with a long, thoughtful gaze as if he had convinced her that his perspective was the right one. Caught her- self batting her eyes.

She could always count on Demetri's grim demeanor whenever he talked about politics, the refugees, and all the small wars worldwide. But he was supercharged whenever he started in about the European Union's relationship with Greece (which he usually did), and his earnest eyes drew her in with the promise of glorious eroticism. During these moments, she imagined them as mad lovers on her tiny, quilted bed: the small bedside lamp rendering them moving silhouettes. He, in tightest black jeans, his white shirt ripped off; she, unclothed, lying in wait, ravenous for what was to come. His massive shoulders fall on her, the hot weight presses against her chest. His roughened, brutish hands reach deep into her hair, cradling her neck and head, and, with his tongue deep, she tastes their mix. The rawness of his masculinity, her femininity. He kneels forward between her legs, his experienced hands work to smooth, to thrill, and he delicately cups her breasts, kisses them, respects their tenderness, burrows his head softly between them. Reaches down to his belt.

"Vera!" he said, glancing from her to the chocolates. His smile was more of a smirk, though, as if he knew she fantasized about him sexually whenever possible. But did he do the same with her? Think of her, fantasize, want her?

On all the rest, though, she was sure (she had seen it), Demetri had other effects. To his friends, his wife, his children, and mere acquaintances, Demetri's words flowed like a revered gospel: an absolute. The soothing sweetness of his voice took on the power of an operatic solo, so splendid and stirring in nature that the audience had no choice but to sit in reverence. Sean would have called it "the Jesus effect," and then pointed out to Vera that *The Last Supper* essentially confirmed that Mary Magdalene and Jesus were lovers. Why else would da Vinci paint them that way? Side by side? They had sex for sure, Sean had once informed her: "Can't you see the sex in this masterpiece, Vera? It's right there. It's everywhere."

Damn Sean. He was right again. She wanted Demetri. Badly. Her lack of sexual desire had evidently been exclusively for Max. And, as Astrid had pointed out, he was a dumbass too.

CHAPTER 23

TASSO & ELEKTRA

We are here to help each other get through this thing, whatever it is.

—Kurt Vonnegut Jr., *Timequake*

For the past month, chatty Elektra had dropped by Vera's cottage every other day. It was early morning, with ominous clouds gathering, and Elektra arrived with the idea of going on a picnic immediately. "We'll bring umbrellas," she said.

"Umbrellas?"

"Okay, so we do a puzzle," said Elektra.

Elektra's happy confidence was generally pleasant to be around, but it always bordered on nervy: the frisky snaps or blasé responses to any ideas different from her own. Then there was the preposterous perfect posture. The rainbow of colorful sheer tops: her bra of the day (completely unnecessary with the size of her breasts) peeking through, and the cutoff, faded jean shorts (with an inseam of one-half inch, including the frayed edge). Vera guessed Elektra could instill envy and fear in her classmates. Anyone, really. Her brother Tasso's company was enjoyable too. The tender perceptiveness. His patience with Elektra's exuberant optimism; his brazen love for his mama and how he subtly sheltered her; and his responses to Demetri, quick-witted and self-disciplined.

Twelve-year-old Elektra and Tasso had not traveled much, other than the occasional ferry excursion to Athens. Back the same day, as the pensions were too expensive for even one over-night. Their understanding of the world was gleaned from the internet and books. They were prisoners of their island: an island education, island playmates, and island expectations—and yet at twelve years old, in the sixth grade, they already seemed to know more than most ever could. They were both inquisitive. But Elektra's responses could be ungrateful and cold. As if whatever you said to her didn't matter because she knew this already. She probably listened to Demetri. At least, this was how Vera saw it.

Elektra and Vera were on the terrace, working on a puzzle of a captivating scene that dotted the island: a brown, scraggly olive tree surrounded by blooming red poppies.

"You look up a lot, Vera," Elektra said, and popped another piece into the puzzle.

"You're a lot like your dad, Elektra."

"I am?"

"You must be popular in school—everyone likes you. Yes?"

A rat-a-tat at the door. So faint, she wasn't sure if anyone was knocking.

"Come in," she shouted.

"Oh, sorry. Interrupt?" Tasso said, his footsteps light, as if he were eternally considerate of someone sleeping.

Without acknowledging Tasso, Elektra picked up another piece and scanned the puzzle.

Vera looked over her reading glasses, pushed halfway down her nose. "Lemonade?"

"Yes. Thank you."

She removed and folded her tiger-patterned glasses, and Tasso passed her a small apricot. "I picked it on my way here."

A bit larger than a golf ball. Soft, fuzzy and still warm from Tasso's hand, Vera held it in her palm and was pleasantly surprised with the apricot's coloring. A splendid mix of color, and she thought of her paint palette. Pink mixed with yellow.

"Lovely. Thank you."

They sat around the table. Vera and Tasso staring at the puzzle with their iced lemonades in hand. Elektra's purple-painted fingernails hovering over the puzzle in a claw position, ready to pounce.

"Mama wants you to come home now," Tasso said to Elektra in English.

He and Elektra spoke in English whenever Vera was present. They said it was to improve their English, but she could see they were simply tired of deciphering what she was trying to tell them and what they were trying to say to her.

"For what? What does she want?" Elektra said.

"Don't know."

"I want to finish puzzle first."

"It's not half done," Tasso said.

"Vera wants to finish it today. Right, Vera?" Elektra said, not looking up.

Vera took a sip of lemonade. Vera had things to do. She had told Elektra so ten minutes before.

"*Baba* said to come home ..."

Elektra looked up. "No ... he's in Athens now. Liar."

Tasso laughed.

"Elektra. If Baba hears you won't do what Mama asked ... he'll be..."

"Be what? Like how he was when ... he gave you the belt?"

There was a sudden drop of silence, as everyone looked around at everything but each other.

Vera's control over her emotions went into overdrive. She was shocked with the possibility that Demetri would do such a thing to quiet, gentle Tasso, but the grieving process had given her some first-hand experience with the benefits of denying the obvious. Demetri? No. Must have been a threat or something. Elektra naturally exaggerates anyway. Right.

"We'll finish it up another time, okay, Elektra?" Vera said, having already deleted what she had just heard about the belt.

In a blink, Elektra's puppy-dog eyes cut Vera down with the eyes of a Rottweiler: unpredictable and unafraid. Elektra's reckless responses could sometimes come across as if she were invincible. And Vera sensed that Elektra was well aware of this: her standing within the family hierarchy; the almighty power she had as a favorite of Demetri.

"I want to finish the puzzle, now," Elektra said, looking at the pieces.

"You like book?" Tasso asked, looking at Vera's book *The Vagrants* on the table.

"Great. Yes."

"What about?"

"China. After Mao died. About a young girl activist and her family. Do you read books in English?"

"If can. Better than on computer," Tasso said.

"Well, you're welcome to borrow any of my books, Tass—"

Elektra interrupted. "Me and Baba read online. Tasso has little corner of books. Funny Tasso." And she covered her mouth and pretended to giggle.

"I get it," Vera said to Tasso. "If it's a special one. Keep it around like an old friend."

"Baba say old way. New way ... computer," Elektra said. "Baba says me and Tasso will get new cell phone soon."

Tasso smiled, and she caught the dark shadow of fuzz above his lip.

With the air of a twenty-first century princess, Elektra elevated her head, scanned the terrace, and said, "I go home now." Shook a few curls away from her face, nodded to Vera, and, on her way out the door, yelled, "I be back tomorrow."

"More lemonade?"

"No. Okay."

"What else do you like besides reading books?"

"Soccer. Music. Poetry sometimes."

"Poetry. Who do you like? Do you want to be a poet someday, Tasso?"

"Only know ... one thing. Don't want to be ... a farmer."

An unease swarmed up inside of her: she might be the first person he had said this to. It was a call for help. As Max liked to say: "You don't have to go to Yale or Hava'd to see that."

"Oh."

She didn't want to go against her Demetri, had never discussed Tasso with him. Pretty obvious to anyone that Demetri
and his son were very different, each almost embarrassed with
one another.

Her voice was shaky. "Have you talked with your father about
it?"

"Makes him sad … angry sometimes."

She gave a nod.

"He cried about it one time. Lots of kitron … with friend
Christos. I could hear from kitchen."

She gave a nod.

Flattening her lips into the Mona Lisa smile, she hoped Tasso
interpreted it as honest concern. Which, of course, it was. So
lovely, this boy. And brave. To go up against what Demetri may
have wanted.

"Only time I hear him cry."

Her smile felt brittle, on the verge of shattering.

"And another time. About Farmers and the EU," Tasso said.

"Yes, it upsets him," she said, relieved that her lips felt all rubbery now and could adapt appropriately to each new revelation.

"Hell to be farmer here. Look at my father. He is fucked up."

She swallowed hard when she heard the f-word. Realized how
grown-up he was for a twelve-year-old boy. Like a little man.

"I need go bag potatoes."

Her lips parted for her to speak. She said nothing.

Gave a nod.

And he was gone.

She picked up the apricot, cupped it in her hand—again,

was taken by the color. She closed her palm around its smooth skin, as if to protect, and thought about Tasso. He needed to talk with someone. Definitely. He had much more he needed to talk about. And she *would* talk with Tasso, but only if it were okay with Demetri.

Perhaps, someday, another regret for Vera.

CHAPTER 24

NIKO

The deplorable mania of doubt exhausts me.
I doubt everything, even about my doubts.

—Gustave Flaubert

She needed to water the orange tree, deadhead the fading red geraniums, and clear the clutter from the patio table. It was the last week in December, sixty-eight degrees, yet she was sweating from the unusually high humidity—so much for the beginning of midwinter on Naxos and the great escape from Boston's snow and ice. The sweating was better, though. Her cell phone was on speaker, and they had been talking for almost an hour.

"Things still magnificent ... I suppose," Sean said.

"Just about."

"So, the grieving part is over? I'm not familiar with these things. Three months now?"

"Three and a half. Getting there."

"Still sad that Warren never said you were special?"

"What? Before he died?"

"... Or clarified you were a Goddamn fool like Sally. Ran into her yesterday. Seemed surprised I was visiting you. She's not so bad, you know."

"So. Flight booked?" Vera turned her face toward the potted geraniums. Reached over and deadheaded one.

"Two weeks from today I'll be in flight."

"Sally mentioned she had found Jesus and—"

Vera cut him off. "What's the exact date and time you will arrive, Sean?"

"January fourth. Will be so good to get outa here and see you, hon. It's thirty-two degrees here. Icy. Anyway, talk soon, ciao."

She clicked off and looked up to see Elektra and Tasso standing around her patio table.

"Hike the Agiossous trail today?" Elektra stated, more than asked.

"Only ten minutes from Pyrgaki to the trailhead," Tasso said. "Long hike, but we only do a part for you."

"Ahhh … how hard is it?"

"Easy," they said in unison.

"Let's go. I already tell Mama," Elektra said, fingering the thin black leather choker around her neck.

Easy footpaths crisscrossed all over mountainous Naxos, and she had trekked a few from village to village by herself. The walks became spiritual endeavors: nothing to do with exercise or getting from point A to point B. Vera classified them as Thoreau's saunterings—a form of art, really—and was not surprised to find they were the most effective way of healing her grief. Yet never would Vera allow herself to think of her walking as therapy. Ambling along alone, she learned how to summon Warren up whenever she wanted. Separate from any distressing images. These were not bursts, but lengthy conversations. He was always there for the taking—buried deep, but so alive within her mind. Like the rat who presses the lever for a reward, she would conjure up Warren over and over each day because of the exquisite comfort it gave her. She talked to him regularly now. Every day, pretty much.

"It's sixteen or seventeen kilometers," Tasso said, as he watched Vera pack her things.

"We stop and go back when you want, Vera," he said, reassuring her.

Into her backpack, Vera stuffed a couple of water bottles, a wide-brimmed canvas hat, a tube of outdated, greasy sunscreen, and a crumbled protein bar that had been carried from hike to hike and never eaten. Once outside the cottage, Vera spritzed everyone with bug spray. Tasso coughed from the abhorrent aerosol. They headed out: Elektra with loose leather sandals flapping; Tasso in grubbed-up running sneakers; and Vera with her worn, trusty hiking boots and high breathability socks guaranteed to prevent blisters.

It was nice. The trail shifted from a narrow dusty road to a marbled path, occasionally bordered by walls of multicolored stacked stones, sometimes at shoulder height. The views of the hilly terrain were wide open, with spotty patches of trees and craggy little brown bushes that gave sharp, prickly stabs if disturbed. These spirited dots gave the land some life, and from above, the sun's steadfast shine and blue boldness brightened the overall mood. There was a static peacefulness to it all—a winsome backdrop to Vera's unusually sprightly mood.

To her delight, no one initiated conversation. To walk and talk had never been part of the agenda. Back home in Newton, she'd sometimes see women out for walks and was always amused at how they never stopped talking and gesticulating. Never. Felt sorry for them. Frustrated that they should ruin a potentially beautiful promenade with their blabbering. Astrid was part of a women's running group, and once, Vera asked her if they talked and ran at the same time. Astrid thought this question was hilarious. "Of course, we do," she had said. "Most of what we say is total bullshit. Turns into a competition—who can talk the most and still keep up. Never trust your running mates."

Elektra was conveniently in the lead, and, in order to be heard or talk to Vera, she would have had to prance along the trail backward. Tasso, always modest, followed closely behind her. They meandered in silence, saw no one for the first hour except for a distant squadron of goats and two fat brown donkeys roaming off the trail (who looked up at them with curiosity and hope, sizing up the possibility of food). Donkeys roamed the island like overgrown dogs. Vera sniffed and caught the stink of fresh donkey dung. With great show, Elektra jerked off the trail, turned around, and held her nose. Niko seemed to pop out of nowhere.

Niko stood to the trailside as if excited to see them, timorous, and uneasy with himself. He needed to round up the donkeys he said. Niko had a secondhand look about him—a consignment sweater, sturdy and clean but washed too many times and on the verge of ragged. He was pudgy, and at that tweeny age when it's unknown whether or not he would stay chubby as he grew. He was a classmate of Tasso and Elektra.

Elektra immediately engaged with him, as if the three had been lost—wandering for days—and had finally encountered another human being.

"Niko!"

Niko's broad, freckled face broke out into a quick smile aimed at Elektra as he petted the smaller donkey's head. He glanced sideways and briefly made eye contact with Tasso. Seemed to force a smile, as if saying: "I'm a good boy, and I do what I'm supposed to do."

"Hey, Niko," Tasso said. "This is Vera. Can we speak English for her?"

Elektra looked at the donkeys, blinked rapidly at them as if considering.

"Great to see you! Your donkeys are so cute. Fat, though. Diet time." Elektra moved closer to Niko, puffed up her chest, smoothed her fingers back and forth, over and in between the tiny bumps of her breasts.

Niko nodded, fixed his eyes on her face.

"I kyria Makris einai toso kaki!" *Mrs. Makris is so mean*! Elektra said and bunched up her face. "She hates me. Gives me the worst grades. Calls on me when I'm not ready. You see that, right, Niko?"

Niko nodded, petting the larger donkey's head: smoothly and delicately, in contrast to what you would expect from his wide, hefty hands.

"She loooooves you, Niko." Elektra puckered her lips, made a big kissing sound.

Niko slowly smiled. Looked down and slightly shuffled his feet. Would have stuck his hands into his front pockets if he'd had them.

"Did you really get a hundred on the math test?" Elektra asked.

Niko smiled broadly at Elektra, his yellowed teeth unusually large. And, as expected, crooked.

"I need to get the donkeys back."

"Can't keep going with us?"

"I'll see you guys on Deftera ..." Niko said, and peeked at Vera. "Monday."

As if in slow-motion, he led away the two belly-bloated donkeys by the slack, corded rope.

Niko was barely out of hearing distance, and Elektra burst out in a gossipy tone: "I feel so bad for Niko."

"Shhhhhh ..." Tasso whispered.

Elektra zeroed in on Vera's eyes. "He's really, really poor. Father is a drunk. Mother died."

"Let's keep going," Vera said. "You first, Elektra."

They rambled for another hour, and Vera, sweaty and light-headed, suggested they head back. For the next two hours, she tried to enjoy the hike, but her thoughts were dominated by Niko. At one point, some of the larger flattened rocks along the paths reminded her of a fishing excursion she'd had with Warren. The stones off-white color was similar to the ones along the riverbeds. It had been a last-minute trip: the two of them driving three hours to fly-fish the streams of New Hampshire. Remembering the comfortable silences between them on that day, Vera suddenly felt a small warm rush of happiness spread inside. She was so grateful it had happened. Grateful she had tagged along that day. Love you, Dad.

Warren's passion was fly-fishing. Always seemed odd, though, a life insurance salesman obsessed with the beauty of nature, sometimes to the point of reciting poems about it. He loved Hemingway's lines from "Big Two-Hearted River":

"His muscles ached and the day was hot, but Nick felt happy. He felt he had left everything behind, the need for thinking, the need to write, other needs. It was all back of him."

When her dad first read this to Sally and her, they were about twelve. She would never forget the reverence in Warren's voice. The way it was for all things related to fly fishing, really. Sally had asked what Hemingway meant by "other needs," and she thought the word back should be replaced with the word, behind: Sally had said she was sure it was a grammatical mistake.

After waving goodbye to the twins, thanking them with a kiss on each cheek, Vera tottered home and sprawled out on the terrace chair, she too with muscles aching, the kind Hemingway and her father must have relished many times over. She undid her ponytail, shook out her hair. Rubbed her feet, changed into a breezy gauze dress with large intersecting black-and-white triangles (picked out for her by Skye at an artisans' festival). At the pink bathroom sink, the word lilliputian came to mind, and she splashed her face with lukewarm water and imagined it was ice cold. Thank God for her box freezer and ice-cube trays.

A newly adopted cat brushed up against her leg. Strays were everywhere, and she liked the boldness of this hefty tiger-colored one. Always eavesdropping, it seemed. More like a dog than a cat: panted with his mouth open, learned how to fetch with a play sardine, and came when called. She went through an array of names: Tiger, Sean, Metis—even Blinky popped up. Settled on

Dr. Cooke. Cookie. She had never sought out Dr. Cooke to thank him for helping Warren. Not even a quick note. Convinced herself he was already well aware of her gratefulness. Though, knew it would have been a thoughtful gesture for a young doctor starting out. She chafed inwardly. For Christ's sake. If Sean were with her, he'd suggest she pull out the guitar, sing the blues, and be done with it. Sean wasn't there, though. Dr. Cooke must know how he saved us. Right, Dad? Right.

Niko. Poor thing. Elektra clearly pitied him. She was annoyed with Elektra's controlling gaiety during the chance meeting, but then, the antics had seemed to make Niko more comfortable. Elektra was only trying to make Niko feel better. Right.

A rap on the door, and she was surprised to see Cora. Following awkward pleasantries, they sat opposite one another at the patio table. Vera's scrambled Greek and their hands were the only way to communicate, so they ended up drinking lemonade and smiling through multiple painful lulls. She wanted a stiff drink. Fuck the lemonade. Excused herself, wanted more ice, she said, scooted around the corner to the kitchenette, poured a double vodka into her drink. Had already sat down when she realized she forgot the ice. Hopefully Cora hadn't understood what she had tried to relay. Charades for ice cubes was more challenging than you might think.

Good God. Cora must be so lonely. To come here, to see me. We can barely communicate. This was Max's reasoning for the divorce: "I'm lonely, Vera," he had said. Ass that he was. Needle dick.

Well, she doubted Cora and Demetri were on the verge of a divorce (this would be too lucky) and wondered if they had great sex, or any at all. Couldn't see it. Well, she wasn't going to be Cora's new buddy, that was for sure. She pitied Cora.

Vera's close buddies were rebels. They protected her and suddenly—alarmingly so—the question of pity came up in relation to herself. Do my friends pity me? Did Warren pity me? Was that why Warren said nothing to her? What would she say to Cora on her deathbed? I've had nothing but pity for you my whole life, Cora. Bye-bye. Or would she say nothing?

Smiling like a fool at Cora, wobbling her head around like a bobblehead doll, she took a sip of the warm spiked lemonade.

Of course, Warren loved her. No need for her to be pitied. She was a changed person: could be a fucking warrior when she fucking needed to be. But still, couldn't crush the thought of being pitied by those she loved. And maybe she loved Warren more than he loved her. Maybe she loved everyone more than they loved her. Excluding Sean.

Suddenly, Demetri stood beside her on the terrace. Cookie rubbed up against his leg. Meowed. He picked the cat up, cradled him in his arms, and smiled. Demetri appeared as enamored with Cookie as the cat was with him. They were on equal standing with each other.

CHAPTER 25

NODE

Facts are stubborn things.

—Alain-René Lesage,
L'Histoire de Gil Blas de Santillane

The hues within Vera's oil paintings said it all. They were new and softly blended, yet separate, dramatic and bold. She had never been happier, and her work reflected this. Experimenting with pastels, brush strokes, pulling, and dabbing, she produced unique colors and textures that gave her work a harmonious feel. Original. Whole. Finished.

Her past silly obsession with promoting celibacy for all women her age seemed a long time ago. Sally would most likely not visit. Skye and Astrid were making plans to come over. And her relationship with Demetri was on a fast track. Life was grand. Until Sean came to visit.

Sean arrived just after the New Year for a week-long visit, and, after only a few days together, they had developed what she believed was a nice routine. Up, up, early, every morning it was. She agreed to try beaching it during the daytime for a while (well before four o'clock). Sean would shepherd her to the beach (before the crowds), sometimes holding her hand, and set up a tentlike contraption (three staked umbrellas in a circle). He always assured her he would make adjustments as needed to keep her out of the sun. "Promise, cross my heart," he would say, and with a finger, outline a big cross in the center of his chest. "Scout's honor," he would say. "Does anybody know what this even means anymore?"

He coaxed her into the sea every day and they swam side by side. Once, some of the kids on the beach had made fun of her big ass in her too-small bathing suit, and Sean pretended he hadn't heard them (she thought this so sweet). They'd take hikes—leisurely, the only way she would agree to it. Sean got her drunk multiple times (she couldn't remember much of this) mixing kitron (the liqueur Naxos was famous for) with all sorts of juices. He'd make his concoctions pretty, with tiny colored-paper umbrellas (part of his hostess gift was a box with hundreds of them) or attach a wedge of freshly picked orange or lemon to the side of a tall glass. Often, dinner was the native spoon-sweet cocktail with a block of graviera cheese. They drank a lot. Agreed there was a non-religious divinity about ambling in nature, with Vera clarifying that for her it was more saunter-ing, and that she had to be by herself to experience it. They ate often, the finest of Greek food (Sean usually prepared it), they talked about things that mattered, and, of course, they laughed and they laughed.

Vera opened up to Sean about her present state of affairs with grieving. It was like a house with many floors, she told him. Each floor had an emotion: deep sorrow, rage, hate, blame, guilt.

"The whole list," she told him. "In the beginning, I could see only one floor at a time. Now, I can see all the floors together at the same time: I can see the whole house. Any emotion can take hold of me at any time but I've learned what floor they come from, and I can always put them back where they belong. I'm feeling more settled, now." Sean then wanted to know how many floors the house had, was it a little house or a mansion—was it in a nice neighborhood? They laughed so hard; Vera almost peed her bathing suit.

It was late afternoon, and they were back from their last outing to the beach—Sean was to fly out the next morning, back to Boston. They sat in the shade on her terrace. Sean was hogging the shade.

She had a nasty sunburn but forgave Sean's broken promise only because it was his last day on Naxos. Silently, she also forgave him for all the times he had dragged her into the surprisingly frigid, salty seawater when she wasn't in the mood. For the fluid-filled blisters on her feet that he assured her would disappear and never did. And he was forgiven for insisting they hike Mount Zeus when her popped blisters hadn't healed properly. "On the way up, we'll see the cave where Zeus grew up," Sean had said. "This'll be fun!" When they had reached the summit, he announced, "Gee, this map makes the hike look a lot shorter and easier than it is. Stupid map."

With all of it, though, the scratching of each shifting sand pebble packed into her crotch, the slow burn spreading over the back of her neck, the brutal hangover from the night before, and the weight gain of what had to be at least ten pounds, Vera still wanted Sean to stay forever.

"Seriously now," Sean said. "What you were talking about with the house floors, having all your feelings mixed up together alongside each other … as one. It's like the block universe idea. The past, present, and future are all happening at the same time. Just in different dimensions and something we earthlings can't navigate yet."

Sean was taking it too far, as usual, and Vera had to reel him in.

"So, the future is … already happening, happened?

"Something like that."

"So, you mean it's already been decided if I save mankind or not?" She blinked her eyes repeatedly.

"Yup."

"Gee. I wonder if I do save the world. Have, or will. Sounds as if I can't do much about it now. How about a nice cold drink, Sean?"

He prepared his favorite yellow kitron cocktail (the one with the highest alcohol content) over ice for both of them. Her computer sat on the terrace table, and Sean asked if he could use it to check on his flight status.

"Can't believe you don't have a password for access to your computer. Woulda thought you'd be terrified of a big ole Greek burglar breaking into your quaint little 'the door's always open' cottage and stealing all your paintings. Don't people here know you are the next Pat de Groot?" Sean chuckled.

"Ha-ha," she said, rolling her eyes. "I got rid of the password because it was super ridiculously long and complicated. Thought it would be easier for Demetri to skip it."

"Demetri?"

"Yes, Demetri. Now don't be jealous—"

Sean broke in. "He doesn't have a computer? I thought you said the government had given every farmer a computer?"

"They did. But Demetri always forgets his. So I let him use mine."

"Whatever. I can see Demetri has his way with you … anytime and anyway he wants," and Sean pretend gasped, both hands on his cheeks.

She laughed. "I've done my best to stand up to him … but hey … it's tough going against a god, you know …"

Sean logged on, and she took a sip of her ice-cold cocktail, the tall glass already sweating from the heat.

"Looks good. I'll need to be out of here first thing tomorrow."

"Aww … I'll miss you …"

"Should I book a flight to Athens too, or do I show up and hope for the best?"

"I'd book."

"Which search engine do you use."

"I only use one … I'm a computer-user wannabe, Sean. You know this."

"Then … why am I looking at so many search engines?"

"Dunno … Sean." And Vera thought for the first time how nice it would be to have the cottage to herself again.

"What the hell?" Sean said, sat back, crossed his arms over his chest, and stared at her.

"Wha …" Vera fired back, made a face, and emphasized the absent letter t with her mouth open wide.

"Wow."

"Wow, what?"

"I'm kinda surprised by this."

She wanted another drink. Just a little more of the yellow magic. More ice too. "Surprised by what?"

"You're into the deep web … the dark web …"

"Excuse me?"

"Like you don't know? Too funny."

"I don't know …"

"You serious?"

"Ya. I'm serious. What do you see?"

Sean leaned in. Positioned his head unusually close to the screen and looked at her from the corner of his eye. He held the stare.

"You have several, what I call … *special* browsers that get you into the … dark net."

"I do?"

"Ya. You do."

"What?" she said. "You mean the web for … I've heard about it…."

"Ya."

"Well … I have no idea how those ended up on my computer."

"Somebody had to download them."

"Well … I didn't."

Sean sat back.

"Must have been your Demetri … your new traveler. Nice, he's so open and honest about what he's doing with your computer."

"If it isn't too much bother … what are you are talking about … what exactly is the dark web?"

"Okay! I'll tell you, and then you can tell me what the fuck Demetri is doing on it … with your computer—if he's such a fucking dummy about computers, as you say."

"Okay. Okay. Relax."

"With the dark web, you're anonymous. You can do a lot of illegal things on it. Buy, sell drugs, sick sex … pedophile shit … basically, people can communicate with each other, do whatever weird shit they want … without being found out."

"Can't all be bad," she said, her hands wet and cold, as she tightened her grip around the iced drink.

"No. Not all of it. It was developed by US intelligence in early 2000 to help their own people communicate … help people living in repressive regimes."

"Is it big? This web?"

"Over five hundred times the size of the surface web … the web you use."

"Oh … so what you're saying is … the dark web is so vast … Demetri could have been exploring anything. He's very curious, you know."

She closed her eyes. Sean, fast and furious, tapped the computer keys.

"Another drink, Sean?"

She got up and drifted from the terrace into the main room of her cottage. At the kitchenette end, she busied herself for a while with the pouring of another kitron liqueur on the rocks—which she didn't even want. Was back in her chair, facing Sean, and halfway through the drink she was forcing down when he finally spoke.

"Well, you're right. He doesn't know much about computers."

"Told you," she said, and took another big gulp. Stared at him with glassy eyes.

"His complete history is intact … he must not know how to delete it. Dummy."

"So … we can see everything he's searched for … on the web …"

"I'll be straight with you. Not good."

"Tell me!"

Sean looked at the screen again.

"Please … please … Sean … don't tell me Demetri is a pedophile … into sick sex …"

"He's not a pedophile. That I'll give you."

"Thank you, dear God."

"… like into some other stuff."

"Like?" She wished she had doubled the kitron. Wanted to be somewhere else.

"Like … bomb shit … how to make a bomb … detonate it. A lot about car bombs … media stories about mass casualties. Vera. Look at me. He's been communicating with some kind of underground group … RAS? Does this mean anything to you?"

Vera raised her palm facing Sean, tried to shield her face. "Stop. Stop it."

"Looks like the farmers and this RAS are teaming up."

"Okay. Okay." She closed her eyes. "I think RAS has something to do with a student revolutionary something or other. Protesting conditions, cuts in the schools and universities."

"Ya. Well, it looks to me as if they are planning some sort of a terrorist attack together."

"What? Demetri and the farmers do things like … block traffic with their tractors."

"Looks as if Demetri's moved up—to the big time."

"No … crazy …"

Sean sat back, meshed his fingers together. "He's using your computer as a node."

"A wha …"

"A node. He's using your computer as a connection point, along with many other nodes, to send things and make the computer route as circuitous as possible—so he can hide his location and identity."

"Totally weird shit, Vera."

"Look," she said. "People are always protesting about something or other here, Sean. Part of being Greek."

"Haven't you talked about this? When it obviously matters so much to him?" Sean asked, with a bewildered frown.

She looked up, ignored Sean's expression. Tried to sound confident with the little knowledge she had. Took an exaggerated swig.

Slowly, Vera said, "I think he made references here and there. Greeks were fools to join the EU. Blah-blah-blah. Dictates from Brussels are destroying the farmer. Greek government does nothing—pretends to be in charge. Blah-blah."

She took another gulp. "Now the migration crisis and Lesbos—farmers think the money will go there."

"What do the farmers want?"

"State subsidies … tax exemptions … respect."

"Well … it looks as if the small-farmer group is hooking up with RAS—a huge and powerful group … and violent."

She tried to articulate her words, but her pronunciations came out ridiculously overdone. "RAS … what do they do … so … violent?" Shook her head, squared her sagging shoulders, tried to move slowly and gracefully, took a sip from her drink.

"What kind of violence?" Sean shot back. "The blowing-up-people kind … banks, government buildings, buses full of people. That kind."

"Well …" she sputtered, "I've told you before! The farmers have only done pee … th … peaceful stuff," she slurred.

"What the fuck? You're drunk. This is serious shit, Vera … look at me! Looks like your marvelous god neglected to tell you what he spends most of his time doing … besides planting and hoeing the potatoes.

"You need to listen up! You've had enough kitron for now …" He pushed her empty glass to the side.

"Weeeell. Hey! Don't get mad at me! I'm not a th … terrorist."

She blinked her eyes and tried to look alert (for Sean's sake), but she was glad to be wasted—her surreal state of mind might cushion the blows of whatever else she was about to hear. And it did.

Demetri planned to bomb a place or kill somebody. Somebody important. Who, what, when, and where, Sean could not decipher from the coded correspondence with someone called Rabbit. Nonetheless, something was imminent.

Demetri's mistake of not deleting his recent history had resulted in careless communication ("so unbefitting a terrorist," Sean had remarked).

Demetri had researched bomb-making extensively, all kinds of bombs. Guns, grenades, plastic explosives. In his last communication with Rabbit, Demetri said he had all the ingredients to finish the rabbit-and-potato stew. He would make the stew, let it simmer, and let him know when it was ready.

CHAPTER 26

TOO MUCH KITRON?

So let us not talk falsely now, the hour is getting late.

—Bob Dylan, "All Along the Watchtower"

The next day, as Sean was about to leave Naxos for Boston on his 6:00 a.m. flight, he suddenly announced at the kitchen door that he wasn't going to leave her alone. He played up the big macho thing (how she saw it) where he was going to confront Demetri and "beat the shit out of him" (those were his exact words). But for all she knew, Demetri might pull a hand grenade from his back pocket and blow Sean up.

"I think it's really weird you never introduced him to me while I was here and all," Sean said.

"It is weird. But you never asked to meet him. Likewise with Demetri."

"If you had initiated a meeting, maybe I would have figured out he wasn't your new traveler but a fucking-crazy terrorist— wouldn't have to leave you with this. But you didn't do it, Vera."

Eventually, she convinced Sean to leave on his flight as planned. Yes, she would contact the police … yes … she would be sure to get a heavy lock for her door. ("This I insist on, Vera," Sean had said.) Yes, Yes, Yes.

Minutes later, she blinked and comprehended the implications of what she now understood about Demetri and immediately faded into a state of stuporous denial. So much so that an hour later, she awoke to find herself still on the terrace, staring at her bare feet burning in the sun. Fucked up again. Should have had Sean meet Demetri. Dad, can you believe all this?

She heard a light rap on her door: not a may-I-come-in, but a here-I-am rap. She looked up to see Demetri on the terrace, smiling at her. It was nine o'clock in the morning.

"Hey," he said, still smiling.

She was mute, stared at him, already seated across from her.

He was *so* sorry to interrupt her ... but he was *so* happy she was writing and having a good day ... and he was *so* interested in how her visit with Sean went ... and she looked *so* much more beautiful now, if this were possible, with her slight suntan ... and what good luck for him she had her computer already out ... forgot his ... and would it be okay if he used it for a minute because he wanted to check his messages, and he honestly didn't know what he would do without her. Pulled the computer to him.

Fucking cocksucker.

And the faint whisper of familiar rumblings returned. Detailed flashes came and went of Nurse Nora, Nelson, even Blinky the dog and the pile of steaming dog shit. But she couldn't speak. Heard Demetri thanking her again for letting him use her computer. He pecked away.

"Liar! I need to get to the US Embassy!" she screamed to herself, and again, her thoughts were taken over by details and doubt.

Demetri tapped away, and her eyes followed his nimble fingers.

She would need a ride to the airport. Bring her computer for evidence. Take the flight to Athens at eleven. It was nine twenty. She would need to leave by ten to make it to the airport—she had half an hour. The unreliable island taxi service would never work.

"You going to Athens today?" she heard herself say.

"Sean visit nice?" Demetri asked.

She opened her mouth to speak. Couldn't hear anything. Jesus fucking Christ, she was waiting too long to respond!

"Hey ... ah ... ah ... I ... ah ... could you drop me off at the airport on your way to the ferry? Want to take the eleven o'clock flight to Athens."

"My ferry leave mesimeri ... *noon* ... agrotika pragmata ... *farmer stuff*," Demetri said, not bothering to look up from the computer screen.

"Ya. I know ... you'd be at the ferry early ... a little."

"Hum ..." Demetri stopped typing.

"Ah, you missing Sean. Too much ... kitron last night?" He patted her hand and smiled gingerly as if he understood that a raging hangover was the cause for her dazed muteness, and he felt her pain.

"Okay, then. You ready go?" he said.

Her head nodded yes.

"See you thirty minutes, my little American." And he looked her in the eyes for the first time. He zeroed in on them and lingered. Maybe for too long.

Alone, she looked up, far beyond the thin shell of bluest sky and rocketed into a startling state of high anxiety. Unbelievable. Dad, he fucking came in here to use me again. Complete cluster-fuck. Sorry for the profanity.

Her first inclination was to call Sean. Then Astrid. A text to Skye? Sally ... ask Jesus for help? Zoom everybody together? Text?

> *Hey! I think one of my dearest friends (okay, I'm practically in love with the guy—did I tell you my sexual drive is back in a big way) who has an abundance of metis, who I truly believed was to be one of my travelers (you remember my lecture on travelers, right?) is a terrorist. And he is planning to set off a bomb or something to cause horrific mass casualties somewhere in Athens. Exactly how, when, and where I have no idea. Let me know what you think!*
>
> *Hope all is well.*
> *Love, Vera*
> *PS I could be altogether wrong about all this.*

As for the local authorities, who would she notify? The island police force was small and they probably couldn't speak English. And even if they did, would only laugh at her, call her crazy—the oversexed Americana whore, always on top, suggesting her lover Demetri, their island god, was a terrorist. And the Greek police on the mainland were out of the question: from what she had read, lots of corruption, with most citizens avoiding them at best. At worst, they would be complicit with Demetri and his group, and she would be in danger. Getting to the US Embassy in Athens was the logical thing to do. Bring her computer for evidence. They'll know what to do.

She comforted herself with the idea that a scheme was already in motion. Demetri would pick her up at ten, and during their forty-five-minute drive to the airport, through casual conversation, she would find out as much as she could about where he went in Athens. Take note of what he was wearing and carrying—overnight bag or backpack. She knew the new plastic explosives didn't take up much space ... fucker. It can't be for today.

She'd surprise him at the airport by taking a photo of him before boarding. Act all happy. Once at the embassy, all she had to do was to tell the story and hand over his photo, pull up his emails. All she had to do was act.

A rap on the door. Elektra stood in front of her. It was nine thirty-five.

At first glance, Vera could see Elektra was preoccupied—more jumpy than usual and repeatedly swallowing with short gasps and gulps, her eyes darting and blinking about.

"You okay, Elektra?"

"Sean leave?"

"About three hours ago."

Elektra seemed to almost flinch.

"You okay, Elektra? Tell me what's going on."

In a whisper, Elektra said, "It's okay." And looked down.

"What's okay?"

"Nothing."

"You can tell me, Elektra. What is it?"

"It's nothing."

And on and on it went, until Elektra finally stopped her crazy breathing pattern long enough to take one good hard look at Vera and see that things weren't right with Vera either. And suddenly, they both knew, they both knew something.

"Vera ...?"

"I'm going to Athens this morning."

"Oh? On the ferry ... today?"

"Ah ... no. Flying. Your father is picking me up at ten. Me and my little red duffle."

Right. Her father is a fucking terrorist (maybe), and it's crucial Elektra knows her travel plans and the color of her bag.

"I should be back tomorrow night. Your father is going to Athens today too, Elektra," she said hurriedly. "I don't mean to be rude ... but I only have about twenty minutes to get my things together before your dad shows up."

Elektra stared at her.

"We'll talk when I get back." And she headed to her bedroom to pack her bag.

Elektra let herself out.

CHAPTER 27

THE PICNIC

Was it his daughter he saw, or his own image gazing back at him?

—Roberto Calasso, *Literature and the Gods*

The same day Vera found out from Sean about the simmering rabbit and potato stew—Demetri, Elektra and Tasso had a picnic. They spoke to each other in Greek.

The plan was so simple. So simple, even twelve-year-old twins could do it.

"Ah. You will make me so proud!" Baba had cried to Elektra and Tasso. It was their third picnic outing together that month.

Mama seemed pleased with the arrangement. "Ah, my three mice are off together again," Cora would crow, waving them off with yet another packed lunch, and beaming as if so proud of her husband, Demetri—good father to her children. Faithful husband to her.

It was late morning. After a ten-minute walk from their home, the three stood at the top of a small, wooded hill with an expansive view of the winding road below. In the shade of an old fig tree, they all sat down cross-legged on a thin, ragged patchwork quilt that once lay on the bed of Cora and Demetri.

Cora had sewn it for her wedding night, bright and beautiful, meant to cover and hide the many future years of her private surrenderings to Demetri, and now, old and faded, the tired quilt had a new life as the family's picnic blanket.

Demetri lightly tapped Elektra's sneaker. "I have a surprise," he said, pulling a cell phone from his backpack. "Baba always keeps his promises to you.

"Here, take it." And he handed it to Elektra.

"Oh, Baba," said Elektra, spellbound. She stared as if transfixed by the push buttons, the orange plastic case. Turned it over and over in her hands. Blinked a smile at Tasso and beamed at Demetri. Waited for further instruction.

"There is evil in the world." Demetri bored his eyes into Elektra's. "You are not too young to understand. The whole lot of European Union bosses are bad, they are evil. They try to suck the life from little people like your Baba. They are not Greek, like us. People in Brussels and Berlin decide how your father should farm his own land. And they will never stop—never. We must stop them. And I need you to help me stop them, Elektra. And you too, Tasso. Will you do this for me? For your Baba?"

"Yes! Yes!" Elektra said with a sudden spurt of energy.

Demetri moved his gaze to Tasso.

"Yes, Baba," Tasso said. "You are our father."

Demetri uncrossed and outstretched his legs, turned to lie on his side, propping his head up with an elbow.

"Ah … what a day …" he cooed. "Such a beautiful day for a beautiful picnic with my beautiful children.

"Are you hungry, my little ones?"

They both nodded.

Elektra carefully lay the cell phone down next to her sneaker on the blanket. Her father motioned for her to open the picnic basket, watched her as she obediently took out three small plates. On each plate, she placed stuffed vine leaves, meatballs, kalamata olives.

And for the next hour, Demetri laughed and joked with his two children, practicing and fine-tuning which strings to tug and how hard, making them each dance for him.

Demetri stood. Spread his arms wide, palms up. "Ah. My beautiful Greek children … ahhh, filotimo … pride in Greece, respect for your elders, we are Greek forever! No one can ever take this away. Filotimo is in our blood," he thundered.

Tasso mostly listened. Looked down at the washed-out quilt beneath him, ran his fingers over and over the many tiny stitches.

"Elektra!" her Baba said, his tone severe, almost frightening.

Tasso was visibly puzzled, his brows furrowed, at the change in his father's tone. He looked up.

"My little lambs! All I need you to do for me is to push buttons on this nice new cell phone."

Demetri bent down, grabbed the cell phone from the blanket; Elektra and Tasso scrambled up to stand.

"Look down to the road," he motioned to the road below. "Christos is helping Baba too. Tomorrow. First, you will see Christos's blue pickup truck. Then you will see my white van following him … on the road."

"When the van is about there … see where the road curves around the cedar bush … do you see it? … all you need to do is press 4-4-4 on the cell phone. Like this." He demonstrated.

"What will happen?"

"A good thing," said Demetri. "For Greek people. For us. The van will blow up."

There was a spell of silence.

"You will be heroes. For Mama—everybody you know," Baba said.

"You won't be in the van, right, Baba?" Elektra asked.

"No. You won't see me in the van at all …"

"Why your van, Baba?"

"My van will be waiting for them when they arrive at the airport. I'll take a taxi to the ferry." He scoffed. "The only decent van on the island … only one good enough for the devils to ride in … I will be on my way to Athens when you are here on the hill tomorrow," Demetri said. "I promise. Christos—in his blue truck—will lead my white van along the road, show them the way to their hotel."

"But … who … who will be in the van when Elektra pushes the buttons?" Tasso asked.

"The devils I told you about. They are flying in on a private helicopter. A group of … European Union Bosses," Demetri sneered. "Pretending to be like us. Pretending to care about us."

"But … who will be driving the van?"

"No one you know. Security ones. You do not know them … you do not know any of them."

"Elektra. *You* push the buttons 4-4-4. Tasso will be there to make sure you do it on time." He tapped Tasso on his shoulder.

Demetri held a finger to his pursed lips. "Shhhhh ... secret between us. Shhhhh ... can you keep the secret with me ... from Mama too?"

"But—" Tasso said.

"For me? Just keep looking at the cell phone for the time. Be here tomorrow at eleven o'clock. Don't be late. On this hill. Bring water."

"Why do—" Tasso said.

"Half an hour after you arrive. You will see the blue truck and van. Eleven thirty."

He handed Elektra the orange phone.

"Put this in your backpack. Do not take it out unless you are checking the time, or you are here with Tasso. Do you understand, Elektra?"

"Will ..."

"No more questions, Tasso. Too many questions. Just do what I say." And he glared at Tasso with flinty eyes.

"Both of you—leave after you push the buttons. Go home."

"Will we see it blow up, Baba?" Elektra asked, looking down at the cell phone in her hand.

"You will do a great thing. Like a hero," Demetri said, and made a tight fist, punched it in the air. "Yes! My Greek heroes of Naxos."

Demetri turned to Elektra. "I know you can do this for me, Elektra," he said. "You are strong, Elektra. Like me. Like your Baba ... like Tasso. We are Greek, Elektra. This means you must be brave. For me. For everybody you know on Naxos. For Greece."

Demetri stepped toward her. He locked her into place with burly arms and cradled her head and pressed it against his chest. She burrowed in.

He pulled slightly on her shoulders with his arms outstretched, held her face directly in front of his.

"Ahhhh ... Elektra—do as I say, and I won't have to send you to the orphanage in Athens!" And Demetri cocked back his head to laugh. Smiling, he circled back to her, his eyes deep empty holes of black.

CHAPTER 28

THE CEDAR BUSH

The open mind never acts; when we have done our utmost to arrive at a reasonable conclusion, we still ... must close our minds for a moment with a snap, and act dogmatically on our conclusions.

—George Bernard Shaw,
"Christianity and the Empire"

If Vera knew what could happen, she might have done things differently. Maybe not. Maybe it's what she wanted all along.

She stood outside her cottage, waiting for Demetri to pick her up. Keep it together. Just get to the embassy. Fucker. Her feelings of anger were somewhat canceled out by the bite of her determination, and this calmed her. But the fitful stabs of fear made her jittery; she refused to look at her hands—the trembling.

It was only ten o'clock in the morning, and the heat of the day had already encroached with the weight of stickiness. Only the scraggly bushes and outcroppings of rock seemed immune. A shiny black beetle scurried under a rock to hide from the sun.

My God. It was the stuff of a harrowing screenplay: on a Greek island, about to carpool with a maybe terrorist. She felt chunks of the unripe banana she had eaten for breakfast frothing around in her stomach, resisting the gradual change into the slushy liquid of gruel. It all suddenly churned upward. She gagged. Tried to focus on the cottage. But her innocent, tiny white cottage, once safely tucked into the cushion of plush petals and perfume, was now devoured by thirsty, creeping greenery: the shoots and stems fitfully entangled. The mugginess seemed almost visible, fluctuating between a green and yellowish tint. She felt faint. Her mouth dry.

A cloud of dust rode in with the wheels of the van as it pulled up; Demetri gave her a big smile. Her anger surfaced. She collected herself. Wanted to sledgehammer the perfect teeth.

A skinny black cat scurried by, crossing in front of the van. Great. Perfect.

"Ahhh … you have not been waiting, I hope," he said to her through the van's open window. His smile went on for way too long. She caught the smell of her own sweat dribbling down her neck and was repulsed at the thought of his sweat mixing with hers. She moseyed to the passenger side, opened the door, threw her leather bag onto the backseat, and climbed in—as if it were another perfect sunny day on the lovely island of Naxos. She caught a glimpse of something big and black in the back seat.

His smile stuck in place, Demetri seemed to make a point of looking her in the eyes without blinking. Odd. He put the van in drive and crept forward.

"Why go to Athens today?" he asked.

"Bank stuff," she said. Hot sweat seemed to be everywhere. Her skirt was too short, and her ass was stuck to the vinyl seat. I can play this game too, dickhead. "And you?"

"Business. Farmer business."

Staring straight ahead, she told herself she was being irrational. Ridiculous to think he knew she knew. Right. Right. She tried to sort out her emotions. Still, it immobilized her to the point of being almost catatonic, and the strategy—periodically interrupting her pre-panic-attack stage to chime in with a word here or there—was going nowhere. A cruel swell of nausea came and went. The seasick kind. The kind she'd had in hospital room 350. And for a brief moment, she felt lost and adrift. The van ceiling had brown stains all over, and she looked up to one, watched how it spun for her like a wind vane. The fierce wind tried to pound and batter her sails from every angle, but she was well versed now: she reefed in the main, started the engine, cut through the waves and the wisps of wind. Okay. Better now. Jesus fucking Christ. Can you believe how he lies to me, Dad?

Craning her neck, she looked in the back seat. There, beside her red bag, lay a black cloth bag, zippered up the middle—looked like a mini body bag to her. The perfect size to carry an Uzi or two.

She turned, looked straight ahead, engaged with the specks of dried dirt on the windshield.

"What's in the big bag?" she said to an unusually large speck.

"Ergaleia! Just tools!"

"Tools for what?"

"Tools to fix things."

"Like what?"

Demetri gave a throaty laugh, the van seemed to slow down.

"Like things—need to be fixed!"

Up until this second, it hadn't occurred to her he could be on his way right now. Good God! On his way *now*—to kill. Maim masses of innocent people … the plan was for today … the fucking rabbit stew was ready. What's in the black bag? Suicide vests? Ice-cold realizations numbed her thoughts, and she nodded up and down as the rhythm inside of her head melted into warm waves. Maddening, infuriating waves—each one deliberating for too long about whether Demetri made any sense. Right. Things that need to be fixed are fixed with tools. What a revelation. Asshole.

The embassy will never have enough time to stop it.

"Have you painted today … yet?"

"No," she panted out. Needed to breathe into a paper bag. The van picked up speed. "No," she repeated.

"Maybe later today, you will?"

Right. Right.

"I know what you're up to. Rabbit stew," she said.

"That so …"

"Ya. That so." And she turned to Demetri's profile, his eyes on the road.

"I won't let you board the ferry," she said.

She watched him tighten his grasp on the steering wheel. He slowed the van down at the curve in the dirt road and pulled over to its side. Turned the ignition off, scratched his head.

"And how will you do that?"

"Scream! Yell that you're raping me or something … you know I will."

"I do know—you will."

"Why kill innocent people?" she screeched.

Demetri's lips flattened.

He lunged at her. One enormous hand cut into the front of her throat, the other coiled round to the back of her head as he worked his fingers hard to crush her trachea. The sudden, direct chop of pain to her neck so stunned her that it took her a while to realize she was being strangled. Without air—the collapsing pressure in her chest stabbed with a vicious pain. Savagely, she scratched like an animal, tore at his hands, tried to gouge out his eyes. And in this space of violence, Vera coexisted with the understanding she would die. And her question was, how long? How long would it take for her to die? No one knows. No one ever does.

Fuck. I'm dying. I'm not ready.

She struggled hard for a full one hundred twenty-one seconds, and it took Demetri a further two hundred ten seconds to finally kill her—five-and-a-half minutes of steady, determined violence. The process of her death was brutal but quick, her final breath strangely serene.

And in this bent warp of time from the here to the there, Vera had the most affecting thoughts she had ever had. She looked up to the giant white wings of the albatross: majestically gliding, waiting for Vera to make her choice. She went with it. Wanted the bright light.

She didn't speak to any God. If her death had been a long, drawn-out affair, she might have searched for, spoken to a greater power. Seriously explored what Buddhism had to offer. Gone over things. Drawn up a to-do list. But her death was so sudden, so fast, so wholly unlike what she had expected (bidding farewell with dignity and grace to all) that she got right to it: narcissistic thoughts. She bypassed the bottomless pit of uncertainty and celebrated herself. She sang her song, fearlessly. Purred with perfect operatic notes. With each comforting rush of enhanced clear thinking, she marveled at herself. So brilliant a human being, she. To have known. To have known her travelers should give such a divine pulse in her death. She loved herself. Her travelers flashed with tantalizing colors. They all loved her. Everlasting. She was completely satisfied in every respect, with an extraordinary freedom from all angst.

Demetri got out, slipped around to the passenger side, looked at his watch. Pulled open the door, snared her ponytail, wrapped it around his hands, and wrenched her to the ground. Let go of her hair. Grabbed her hands, dragged her body behind the ragged cedar bush in the road's curve. Spread her out flat. Arms by her side. Her face up. He paused. Crouched beside her and looked into her open eyes. Pushed the lids down.

He bolted back to the driver's seat. Wiped his brow. Started up the van.

What Demetri did not know was that Elektra and Tasso had arrived early. Standing on the hill, they had watched him drag her lifeless body from the van.

Elektra froze, and the cell dropped from her hand. Slowly, Tasso picked it up. He paused. With focused determination, he pressed 4-4-4. The white van below exploded into an orange ball of fire.

Nonfiction books and articles that helped to shape my novel, *Gray*:

Beaton, Roderick. *Greece: Biography of a Modern Nation*. London: Penguin, 2020.

Byock, Ira. *Dying Well*. Penguin, 1998.

Darcy, Susan. *Athena*. London, New York: Routledge, 2008.

Nuland, Sherwin. *How We Die*, 7th ed. New York: Knopf, 1994.

Perkin, RM, and DB Resnik. "The agony of agonal respiration: Is the last gasp necessary?" *Journal of Medical Ethics* 28 (2002): 164-169.

Spathis, Costas. *Greece by Drone*. First edition. Athens, Greece: Proto Thema Publishing, 2019.